Rumpelstiltskin
and Other Grimm Tales

CAROL ANN DUFFY

illustrated by Markéta Prachatická

faber and faber

First published in 1999
by Faber and Faber Limited
3 Queen Square London WC1N 3AU

Photoset by Faber and Faber Ltd
Printed in England by Clays Ltd, St Ives plc

A CIP record for this book
is available from the British Library

ISBN 0-571-19631-4

2 4 6 8 10 9 7 5 3 1

Contents

Hansel and Gretel, 1

The Golden Goose, 21

Ashputtel, 30

Sweet Porridge, 48

Iron Hans, 51

The Musicians of Bremen, 69

The Lady and the Lion, 79

The Fox and the Geese, 92

Little Red-Cap, 94

Two Households, 102

The Hare and the Hedgehog, 104

Clever Hans, 111

Snow White, 120

Brother Scamp, 138

Rumpelstiltskin, 161

The Magic Table, the Gold-Donkey
and the Cudgel in the Sack, 169

Hansel and Gretel

It was no more than once upon a time when a
poor woodcutter lived in a small house at the
edge of a huge, dark forest. Now, the woodcutter
lived with his wife and his two young children –
a boy called Hansel and a little girl called Gretel.
It was hard enough for him to feed them all at
the best of times, but these were the worst of
times; times of famine and hunger and starva-
tion, and the woodcutter was lucky if he could
get his hands on even a simple loaf of bread.
Night after hungry night, he lay in his bed next
to his thin wife, and he worried so much that he
tossed and he turned and he sighed and he mum-
bled and moaned and he just couldn't sleep at all.

"Wife, wife, wife," he said to Hansel and Gretel's stepmother, "what are we going to do? How can we feed our two poor children when we've hardly enough for ourselves? Wife, wife, what can be done?"

And as he fretted and sweated in the darkness, back came the bony voice of his wife, a voice as fierce as a famine. "Listen to me, husband," she said. "Tomorrow at first light we'll take the children into the forest, right into the cold, black heart of it. We'll make a fire for them there and give them each one last mouthful of bread. Then we'll pretend to go off to our work and we'll leave them there all by themselves. They'll never be able to find their way back home on their own. We'll be rid of them for good and only have to worry about feeding ourselves."

When the woodcutter heard these hard, desperate words he said, "No, no, wife, I can't do that. How could I have the heart to leave young Hansel and Gretel in the forest? The wild beasts would soon sniff them out and eat them alive."

But his wife was determined. "You fool!" she

said with tight lips. "Do you want all four of us to starve to death? You might as well start smoothing the wood for our coffins." And she gave the poor, heartsore woodcutter no peace until he agreed to do as she said.

"But I feel so sorry for my helpless little children," he wept. "I can't help it."

Now Hansel and Gretel had been so hungry that night that they hadn't been able to sleep either, and they'd heard every cruel word of their stepmother's terrible plan. Gretel cried bitter, salt tears, and said to Hansel, "Now we've had it."

But Hansel comforted her. "Don't cry, Gretel. Don't be scared. I'll think of a way to save us."

And when their father and stepmother had finally gone to sleep, Hansel got up, put on his coat, opened the back door, and crept out into the midnight hour. There was bright, sparkling moonlight outside and the white pebbles on the ground shone like silver coins and precious jewels. Hansel bent down and filled his empty pockets with as many pebbles as he could. Then he went back inside and said to Gretel, "Don't worry, Gretel, you can go to sleep now. We'll be fine, I promise." And he climbed into bed.

At dawn, before the sun had properly got up, their stepmother barged in and woke the two children. "Get up, you lazy scraps; we're going to the forest to chop wood." Then she gave each of them a pathetic portion of bread. "There's your lunch; think yourselves lucky, and don't eat it all at once, because there's nothing else."

Gretel put the bread in her apron pocket, because Hansel's pockets were stuffed with pebbles. Then the whole family set off along the path to the forest. Hansel kept stopping and looking back towards the house, until finally the woodcutter called to him, "Hansel, what are you dawdling behind for and looking at? Keep up with the rest of us."

"Sorry, Father," said Hansel. "I was just looking back at my white kitten. It's climbed up on to our roof to mew goodbye."

"You stupid boy," said his stepmother, "that's not your kitten. It's just the morning sunlight glinting on the chimney. Now get a move on."

But, of course, Hansel hadn't been looking at anything at all. He'd been dropping a trail of white pebbles on to the path.

The forest was immense and gloomy. When they had reached the middle the woodcutter said, "Now, Hansel, now, Gretel, fetch some wood and I'll start a nice fire to keep you both warm."

Hansel and Gretel gathered a big pile of firewood, and when it was lit and the flames were like burning tongues, their stepmother said, "Lie down by the fire and rest. We're going further into the forest to chop wood. When we've finished working, we'll come back and get you."

The children sat by the fire, and when lunchtime came they nibbled on their small pieces of bread. They could hear the chops of a woodcutter's axe nearby and they thought that their father was close. But it wasn't an axe, it was just a branch that he'd tied to an old withered tree and the wind was blowing it to and fro, to and fro. After they had waited and waited and waited, the children's eyes grew as heavy as worry and they fell fast asleep.

When at last they woke up, it was already bat dark, darker than a nightmare. Gretel started to cry and said, "How will we find our way out of this gigantic forest?"

Hansel tried to cheer her up. "Just wait a bit till the moon rises, Gretel, then we'll find our way home all right." And when the moon had risen, casting its brilliant, magical light, Hansel took his little sister's hand and followed the pebbles. They shone like newly minted coins, like cats' eyes, like diamonds, and showed them the way.

They walked all through the night, and at daybreak they knocked on the door of their father's house. When their stepmother opened it and saw Hansel and Gretel standing there, she snapped, "You naughty brats! Why did you sleep so long in the forest? We thought you were never coming back." But their father was glad to see and touch them again, for he'd been grief-stricken and guilt-ridden at leaving them all alone in the forest.

Not long afterwards, times became very hard once more and the famine bit deeply and savagely into their lives. One night, when they all shivered in bed with empty stomachs, the children heard their stepmother's ravenous voice again, "There's no more food left except a hunk of stale bread, and when that's gone that'll be the end of the lot of us. The children must go, I tell you. First thing tomorrow, we'll take them even deeper, deeper, right into the belly of the forest, so they won't possibly be able to find their way home. It's our only chance to save ourselves." And although the woodcutter became very upset and thought that parents should share their last crumb with their children, his wife wouldn't listen to a word he said. Her sharp voice pecked on and on at him, "You did it before, so you'll do it again. You did it before so you'll do it again." And in the end, the poor starving woodcutter gave in.

Once more, Hansel waited till his parents fell asleep, and then he got up and tried to sneak out like the last time. But the stepmother had locked, bolted and chained the door and Hansel couldn't get out, no matter how hard he tried. He had to go back to bed with nothing and comfort his little sister. "No more tears, Gretel," he said. "Just try to sleep. I know somehow I'll find something to help us."

It was very, very early when the stepmother came and shook the children out of bed. She tossed them each a piece of bread, but they were even tinier pieces than before. On the way to the forest, Hansel crumbled his bit of bread in his pocket, and kept stopping to drop a crumb on the path. "Hansel, why do you keep stopping and looking behind you?" said the woodcutter. "Hurry up."

"I'm just looking back at my pet dove, Father," said Hansel. "It's sitting on our roof flapping goodbye to me."

"You idiotic boy!" snapped his stepmother. "That isn't your dove. It's the sun shining on the chimney." But carefully, tiny crumb after tiny crumb, Hansel laid a rosary of bread on the path.

Now the stepmother had led the children right into the deepest, densest part of the forest, to where they had never been in their whole lives. A big, licking fire was lit again and she told them, "You pair sit and wait, and go to sleep if you get tired. Your father and I are going off to chop wood. When we're finished this evening we'll come and fetch you."

After a while, Gretel shared her miserly lump of bread with Hansel, who had scattered his piece on the ground. Then they fell asleep, and the long evening passed, but nobody came to take them home. The night grew darker and darker, and when they woke up it was too black to see a thing. "Don't worry, Gretel," said Hansel. "When the moon rises, we'll see the breadcrumbs I dropped. They'll show us our way." As soon as the full moon came, glowing and luminous, the two children set off.

But they didn't find a single breadcrumb, because all the hundreds of birds that fly and swoop in the forest had pecked them away and swallowed them. Hansel said to Gretel, "Don't panic, we'll find the way on our own." But they didn't find it. They walked all night and all the following day, and by the next evening they were hopelessly lost in the bowels of the forest. What's worse, they were hungrier than they had ever been in their skinny young lives, because they had nothing to eat except for a few berries they'd managed to find. Eventually, the poor children were so weak and exhausted that their legs couldn't take one step further. So they dropped down under a tree and fell into a deep sleep.

It was now the third morning since they had seen their father. The famished, thirsty children forced themselves to walk on, but they were only swallowed further and further into the forest, and they knew that unless they found help very soon they would die of hunger. When it was midday, they saw a beautiful white bird singing on a branch, and the bird's song was so enchanting that Hansel and Gretel stopped to listen to it. As soon as its song was over, the bird flapped its creamy wings and flew off in front of them, and they followed it till it landed on the roof of a little house.

 When Hansel and Gretel came near, they saw that the house had bread walls and a roof baked of cake and sparkly windows made of clear, bright sugar.

"Look at that!" cried Hansel. "This will do us! What luck! I'll try a slice of roof, Gretel, and you can start on a window. I bet it'll taste scrumptiously sweet."

Hansel stretched up and broke off a bit of the roof to see what it tasted like, and Gretel snapped off a piece of window-pane and nibbled away. Suddenly, they heard a weird little voice calling from inside,

"Stop your nibbling, little rat,
It's my house you're gnawing at."

But the chomping children chanted,

"We're only the wind going past,
Gently blowing on roof and glass."

And they just went on munching away. Hansel reckoned the roof was absolutely delicious and pulled off a great slab of it. Gretel bashed out a whole window-pane and sat down and had a wonderful chewy time.

Then, suddenly, the door creaked open and an old, old woman, bent double on a stick, came creeping out. Hansel was frightened and Gretel was terrified and they both dropped what they were holding. But the old woman wagged her wizened head and said, "Well, well, you sweet little things, how did you get here? Come in and stay with me. You'll come to no harm." She took the children by the hand and led them into the mouth-watering house. Then she gave them a wonderful meal of creamy milk and melt-in-the-mouth pancakes, with sugar and chocolate and apples and nuts. After Hansel and Gretel had scoffed twice as much as was wise, she made up two soft, comfy little beds with the best white linen, and Hansel and Gretel lay down to sleep.

But the old woman was only pretending to be kind, for she was really a cruel and evil witch who lay in wait for children and had only made her bread house with its cake roof to trap them. When a child fell into her bony clutches, she would kill it, cook it, salt it and eat it, and such a day was her favourite gorging-day. Witches have red eyes which they can't see very far with, but they have a powerful sense of smell, as good as a bloodhound's, and they can sniff out anyone who comes near them. So as Hansel and Gretel had wandered nearer and nearer to her little house in the woods, she'd cackled a spiteful laugh and wheezed nastily, "Here's two for my witch belly who shan't escape."

Early next morning before the children had woken, she was already hovering by their beds looking greedily down at them. They looked so sweet lying there with their rosy cheeks that she drooled to herself, "These will make tasty mouthfuls for me to gobble." Then she grabbed Hansel with her long claws and dragged him off to a little shed outside and locked him up behind the door with iron bars. Hansel screamed his head off, but it was useless. Then the witch went to Gretel and poked her awake with her stick and shrieked, "Get up you lazy ingredient! Boil water and cook a meal for your brother. He's locked up outside in the shed and I want him fattened up. When he's good and plump, I'm going to eat him."

Gretel's tears were hot and stinging, but it was

no good, she had to do as the wicked witch said.

Day after day after day, the best meals were cooked for Hansel, while poor Gretel had to live on crabshells. Each morning, the vile witch groped and fumbled her way out to the shed and screamed, "Hansel, stick out your finger for me to feel if you're plump."

But clever Hansel poked out a little chicken bone instead, and the old crone's red witchy eyes couldn't see it. She thought it was Hansel's finger and was furious and puzzled that he went on and on not getting plump. After four weeks of this, she lost her patience completely and refused to wait one day more. "Right, Gretel," she shouted. "Get busy and cook him his last meal. Tomorrow, whether he's plump or skinny, fat or thin, I'm going to slit Hansel's throat with my sharpest knife and cook him."

Gretel sobbed and wailed as the witch forced her to carry the water for boiling, and her face was basted with tears. "Who can help us now?" she cried. "If only the wild animals had eaten us in the forest, then at least we'd have gone together."

"You can cut that bawling out," said the witch nastily. "It won't do you any good."

Next morning, Gretel had to go out and hang up a big cooking pot of water and light the fire.

"First we'll bake some bread," said the witch. "I've already heated the oven and kneaded the dough." She pushed and pinched poor Gretel over to the oven, where greedy flames were already licking at the air. "Crawl inside and tell me if it's hot enough for the bread to go in."

And the witch's dreadful, gluttonous plan was to shut the oven door once Gretel was inside, so she could roast her and eat her as a starter. But Gretel guessed this, and said, "I don't know what to do. How can I get in there?"

"You foolish goose," snapped the witch. "The opening's big enough for you. I could fit into it myself. Look." And the witch hobbled up and poked her potato head into the oven. Then Gretel gave her such a push, such a massive shove, that she fell right into the middle of the oven. Gretel slammed the iron door shut with shaking hands and bolted it. The witch started to shriek and howl in the most appalling way, but Gretel fled outside and the heartless witch burnt agonizingly to death. The smell of roast witch was disgusting.

Gretel ran straight to Hansel's shed and opened it, yelling, "Hansel, we're saved! We're saved! The old witch is dead."

Hansel flew out, free as a bird released from a

cage, and they both danced and cheered and hugged and kissed. There was no need to be afraid any more, so they went into the witch's house and opened all her drawers and cupboards, which were stuffed to bursting with pearls and precious jewels. "These are much better than pebbles," smiled Hansel.

He crammed his pockets with as much as they could hold, and Gretel said, "I'll take some home, too," and filled her apron up to the brim.

"Right," said Hansel, "let's get out of this witchy forest for good."

When the children had walked for a while, they came to the banks of a big, wide river.

"There's no bridge," said Hansel. "We won't be able to get across."

"And there's no boat either," said Gretel. "But look! There's a white duck swimming along. I'm sure it'll help us across if I ask it nicely." So she sang out,

"Excuse me, little white duck,
Gretel and Hansel seem to be stuck.
A bridge or a boat is what we lack,
Will you carry us over on your back?"

Sure enough, the duck came swimming and quacking towards them, and Hansel jumped smartly on its back and told Gretel to sit behind him.

But sensible Gretel said, "No. That'll be too heavy for the duck. I think it should take us across one at a time." And that is exactly what the kind little duck did.

So Hansel and Gretel walked happily on, and the wood became more and more familiar, until at last they saw their father's house in the distance. They began to run, run, run, charged into the kitchen and flung their arms round their father's neck. The poor, sorrowing man had not had one happy moment since he had abandoned his children in the forest, and his wife had died and was buried. But now Gretel shook out the contents of her apron, making diamonds and emeralds and rubies twinkle and shine upon the floor, and young Hansel chucked down fistful after fistful of creamy pearls from his pockets. It was certain that all their troubles were over, and the thankful woodcutter and Hansel and Gretel lived on together at the edge of the forest and were happy ever after.

So that was that. Look! There goes a rat. Let's catch it and skin it and make a new hat!

The Golden Goose

Once there was a man who had three sons. Everyone reckoned that the youngest son was a simpleton. They called him Dummling, and picked on him, sneered at him, and teased him every chance they got.

One day, the eldest lad decided to go into the forest and chop wood there. Before he set off, his mother gave him a fragrant, sweet home-baked cake and an excellent bottle of wine, in case he needed to eat or drink. When the eldest son entered the forest, he saw a wee grey-haired old man who called out good morning to him and said, "Please give me a piece of that cake in your pocket, and let me have a gulp of your good wine. I am so hungry and thirsty."

But the clever son replied coolly, "Certainly not. If I give you my cake and wine, I'll have none left for myself and that wouldn't be very smart, would it? Scram!" And he turned his back on the little man and strode smartly on.

But when he began to chop at his first tree, it was only a few moments before he made a clumsy stroke with the axe, and cut himself painfully on the arm. So he had to hurry home, bawling, and have it bandaged. And it was the wee grey man who had made this happen.

Soon after that, the second son decided to go to the forest; and his mother gave him, too, a delicious cake and a bottle of the best wine. The wee grey man met him as well, and asked him for a slice of cake and a swig of wine. But the sensible son refused. "That's out of the question. Anything I give to you means less for me and where's the sense in that? Hop it!" And he left the old man standing there and walked on shrewdly.

But his punishment was quick. As he was hacking away at a tree, he hit himself in the leg so severely that he had to be carried home, snivelling.

Then Dummling said, "Father, please let me go and cut wood in the forest."

His father sighed and tutted, "Your brothers have hurt themselves already doing that. Be quiet, Dummling. You don't know what you're talking about."

But Dummling begged and pleaded for so long that eventually his father gave in and said, "All right then, go! And when you've mutilated yourself, perhaps you'll learn your lesson."

Dummling's mother gave him a tasteless cake made with water and baked in the ashes and a bottle of sour beer to wash it down with. When he got to the forest, the wee grey man came up to him and greeted him, "Give me a bite of your cake and a swallow from your bottle. I am very hungry and thirsty."

Dummling answered simply and honestly, "I've only got a flour-and-water cake and some stale ale; but if that's good enough for you, you're welcome to share it with me." So they sat down together, and when Dummling took out his ashy cake it was now a superb chocolate cake, with plums in it, and his flat beer had turned into the finest of vintage wines.

They munched and sipped, tippled and chewed cheerfully, and afterwards the wee grey man said, "Since you have such a kind heart, and share what little you have so generously, I am going to give you the gift of good luck. See that old tree over there? Chop it down and you will find something at its roots." Then the old man left Dummling alone.

Dummling ran straight over to the tree and cut it down, and when it fell there was a goose nesting in the roots with feathers of pure gold. He lifted her out, tucked her firmly under his arm, and strode off to an inn where he intended to stay the night.

Now, the landlord of this inn had three daughters, and as soon as they clapped eyes on the goose they were fascinated by it, and desperate to find out what kind of wonderful bird it was. And they ended up by longing for one of its golden feathers. The eldest thought, *I'll be smart and wait for a good moment and then I'll pull out one of its feathers for myself.*

As soon as Dummling had gone out, she grabbed the goose by its wing. But her fingers and hand stuck to the goose like glue. Soon afterwards, the second sister came along with exactly the same bright idea of plucking out a golden feather all for herself. But no sooner had she touched her older sister than she stuck to her.

Last of all, the third sister arrived, hellbent on taking a feather; but the other two screamed out, "Stay away! For heaven's sake stay away!"

But the third sister didn't see why she should be the only one to miss out, and thought, *If they're doing it, I'm doing it*, and rushed over to them. Of course, the moment she'd touched her sister she was stuck to her. And there the three of them had to stop all night: glum, gormless and glued to the golden goose.

The next morning, Dummling tucked the goose under his arm and set off into the wide world, without so much as blinking a blue eye at the three sisters who were stuck behind him. The silly trio had to run after him, any old way he chose to go: left, right, fast, slow, upsy, downsy, round the corner, wherever his legs carried him.

As they were crossing the fields, the parson noticed them, and when he saw the procession following Dummling, he said sternly, "You should be ashamed of yourselves, you disgraceful articles, chasing after a young man through the field like this. What are young girls coming to these days?" At the same time, he grasped the youngest by the hand and tried to yank her away. But as soon as his pious hand touched her young one, he was stuck like the stickiest glue, and had to run after them till his face was redder than shame.

Next thing, the sexton came along and seeing the highly respectable parson, that pillar of the community, high-tailing it after three lasses, he was very shocked indeed and called out, "Hoy, your reverence, where are you haring off to? Have you forgotten we've got a christening today?" He cantered after him and grabbed at his sleeve, but was stuck to it at once.

While the five of them were jogging like this, one behind the other, two workers from the fields went past with their hoes. The parson shouted to them and begged them to help set him and the sexton free. But no sooner had they touched the sexton than the two of them became firmly stuck, and now there were seven of them running behind Dummling and his golden goose.

Eventually, they all fetched up at a city. The King who ruled there had a daughter who was so serious that nothing and no one could make her laugh. Because of this the King had sworn that whoever could make her laugh could marry her – simple as that. When Dummling heard about this, he went straight to the King's daughter with his goose and the parade of seven folk behind him. The po-faced Princess took one look at them all, running up and down as Dummling pleased, and burst out laughing. And she laughed so much it looked like she'd never stop!

Quick as a flash of gold, Dummling asked to marry her, as was his right, and soon enough the peals of laughter became peals of wedding-bells. The wedding was celebrated at once; and Dummling became heir to the kingdom and lived long and happy ever after with his smiling wife.

Ashputtel

One dark time, there was a rich man whose wife became fatally ill. When she felt that the end of her life was very near, she called her only little daughter to her bedside and said, "My darling girl, always try to be good, just like you are now, and remember to say your prayers. God will take care of you and I will watch you from heaven and protect you." When she'd said these words, she closed her loving eyes and died. The young girl went out every day to cry beside her mother's grave. When winter came, the snow was like a white shroud on the grave, but by spring there were flowers embroidered there and the girl's father remarried.

His new wife brought her two daughters to live with them. Although their faces were as lovely as flowers, their hearts were as ugly as

thorns. And so a time of real misery began for the poor little stepdaughter.

"Why should this eyesore sit next to us at supper?" the stepsisters squawked. "Those who want to eat bread must work for it. Get to the kitchen, kitchen-maid!"

They stole Ashputtel's pretty dresses and made her wear an old grey smock and forced her perfect feet into wooden clogs. "Ooh, la-di-da!" they sniggered. "Doesn't the proud Princess look elegant today!" Their bright, mean eyes gleamed, and they laughed at her and shoved her into the kitchen. She had to do all the hard and heavy work from dawn till dusk – get up before the sun, fetch water, make the fire and do the cooking and washing.

As well as all this, her stepsisters bullied her and scattered peas and lentils into the ashes, then forced her to kneel there and pick them all out. At night, when she was completely worn out and exhausted with this slavery, she was given no bed to sleep in like the others, but had to lie down on the ashes by the hearth. And because this covered her in a blanket of dust and grime and made her look dirty, they called her "Ashputtel".

One day, the father was going to the market-fair and he asked his two stepdaughters what they would like as a present.

"Beautiful dresses," said one.

"Pearls and sparkly diamonds," said the second.

"What about you, Ashputtel?" he said. "What would you like to have?"

"Father, break off the first twig that brushes against your hat on the way home and bring it to me."

So he purchased fine dresses and precious stones for the two stepsisters; and on his way home, as he was trotting through a wood, a hazel twig scraped his head and snagged on his hat. He snapped off the twig and put it in his pocket. As soon as he got home, he gave his stepdaughters what they had demanded – how their eyes widened! – and to Ashputtel he gave the twig from the hazel bush.

Ashputtel thanked him, went out to her mother's grave and planted the twig there. She was so unhappy and cried so much that her tears watered the twig as they fell, and it grew into the most beautiful tree. Three times every day Ashputtel went to the tree and wept and said her prayers. Each time, a small white bird came and perched on the tree; and whenever Ashputtel wished for something, the bird would drop it, whatever it was, at her feet.

Now, it happened that the King decided that his son must choose a bride, so he announced that a feast would be held. It was to last for three whole days and all the fine young girls in the country were to be invited. When the two stepsisters heard that this included them, they were thrilled, and their eyes shone and their neat feet tapped with excitement. They called Ashputtel and said, "Comb our hair, brush and polish our shoes and fasten our buckles. We're going to the wedding-feast at the royal palace."

Ashputtel did as they ordered, but she cried because she wanted to go to the dance as well. She begged her stepmother to let her go, but her stepmother sneered, "You kitchen tramp! Look at yourself. Do you want to go to the feast all dusty and grimy? You haven't any frocks or shoes, so how do you think you can go dancing, you scullery slut?"

But when Ashputtel kept pleading and pleading, her stepmother finally said, "See here, I've poured this bowl of lentils into the ashes. If you can pick out all the lentils again in two hours, then you can come with us to the dance."

Ashputtel went through the back door into the garden and sang out,

"Gentle doves and turtle-doves, all you birds of the sky come and help me sort out my lentils:
Into the pot if they're fit to eat,
But swallow the bad ones with your beak."

Then two white doves flew in through the kitchen window, and behind them came the turtle-doves, and then all the birds of the air came

swooping and crowding in and hopped on the floor round the ashes. The doves nodded their small heads and began — peck, peck, pick, pick — and then the other birds joined in — pick, pick, pick, peck, peck, peck — and put all the good lentils into the bowl. They were so speedy and efficient that they'd finished within the hour and flown back out of the window. Ashputtel rushed to show the bowl to her stepmother, bursting with happiness at the thought of going to the wedding-feast. But her stepmother said, "No, Ashputtel, you've got no gown and you can't dance. They'll only laugh at you." When Ashputtel burst into tears, she said, "If you can sort out two bowlfuls of lentils from the ashes in one hour, you can come with us." *She'll never manage that*, thought the stepmother to herself as she emptied two bowlfuls of lentils into the ashes, *it's impossible!*

Ashputtel went out into the garden and called,

"Gentle doves and turtle-doves, all you birds of the sky, come and help me sort my lentils: Into the pot if they're fit to eat, But swallow the bad ones with your beak."

37

Once again, the white doves, then the turtle-doves, then all the many birds of the sky came skimming and swirling in and peck-peck pecked all the good lentils into the bowls. And this time, it wasn't even half an hour before they'd finished and scooted out of the window. Ashputtel took the bowls straight to her stepmother, breathless and overjoyed at the thought of going to the feast. But her stepmother snapped, "It's no good. You can't come because you haven't any fine dresses, you haven't any shoes, you can't dance and we'd all be ashamed of you." And she turned her tombstone back on Ashputtel and marched off with her two proud daughters.

When everybody had gone and the house was empty, Ashputtel went to her mother's grave under the hazel tree and called out,

"Shake your leaves and branches, little tree,
Shower gold and silver down on me."

And the white bird threw down a golden and silver dress and a pair of slippers embroidered in silk and silver. Quick as a smile, Ashputtel put it all on and sped to the feast. She looked so beautiful in the golden gown that her stepsisters and stepmother couldn't see that it was Ashputtel and decided she must be a princess from a foreign land. Ashputtel, they thought, even as they devoured this gorgeous girl with their eyes, was crouched at home in the dirt, squinting, sneezing, and sieving lentils out of the ashes.

The Prince came over to her, bowed deeply, took her hand and danced off with her. He wouldn't let go of her hand, or dance with anyone else; and if another man came up and asked her to dance, he said, "She is *my* partner."

Ashputtel danced till it was evening, and then she wanted to go home. But, because the Prince was desperate to find out whose beautiful daughter she was, he announced, "I shall come with you and walk you home." But Ashputtel managed to slip away from him and hid up in the dovecot. The Prince waited until her father came home, and told him that the lovely, mysterious girl had jumped into the dovecot.

The father thought, *Could she possibly be Ashputtel?* So he sent for the axe and the pick and broke into the dovecot. It was empty. Ashputtel had

jumped down from the other side and run to the
hazel tree. She'd pulled off her dreamy clothes
and folded them on her mother's grave and the
white bird had taken them away. Then she had
crept back to the kitchen in her old grey smock.
When the others came indoors, they saw only
grubby little Ashputtel lying among the ashes in
her dirty clothes, with a dim little oil-lamp guess-
ing in the darkness.

Next day, the second day of the feast, when
everyone had left, Ashputtel went to the hazel
tree and said,

"Shake your leaves and branches, little tree,
Shower gold and silver down on me."

This time, the bird dropped down an even more amazing dress than before; and when Ashputtel arrived at the feast, everyone gaped wide-eyed at her beauty. The Prince had been waiting only for her. He took her by the hand at once and danced with her and nobody else. "She is *my* partner," he said to any man who came near her.

When evening came and it was time for her to leave, the Prince followed her, watching which house she would enter. But she managed to lose him and ran into the garden behind the house, where there was a fine big pear tree in full fruit. She shot up it like a silver squirrel and hid in its branches. The Prince hadn't a clue where she was. When her father came, he said, "That strange, nameless girl has given me the slip again. I think she must have jumped into the pear tree."

The father thought, *Could it possibly be Ashputtel?* So he sent for the axe again and chopped down the tree, but there was no one in it. And when they all went into the kitchen, there was

Ashputtel curled up in her ashes as usual. She'd jumped down from the far side of the tree, given her fancy clothes back to the bird, and dressed in her grubby grey smock again.

On the third day, when her parents and step-sisters had left, Ashputtel went again to her mother's grave and spoke to the hazel tree,

"Shake your leaves and branches, little tree,
Shower gold and silver down on me."

This time, the white bird threw down a dress so sparkling and brilliant that the like of it had never been seen before, and the slippers were golden all over. When she appeared at the wed-ding-feast in this wonderful costume, everyone was speechless with admiration and wonder. The Prince danced only with her, and if anyone else asked her for a dance, he said, "She is *my* partner."

When evening came, Ashputtel wanted to leave, and, even though the Prince wanted to come with her, she dashed away from him so fast that he couldn't keep up. But this time, the Prince had thought of a trick. He'd had the whole staircase covered with tar, and as she rushed down it, her left slipper got stuck there. The Prince picked it up and looked at it closely. It was small and delicate and pure gold.

The next day, the Prince took the slipper to the house of Ashputtel's father and said to him, "I will only marry the girl whose foot fits into the golden slipper."

Ashputtel's two sisters were thrilled because they had beautiful feet. The eldest took the shoe up to her bedroom to try on, with her mother breathing down her neck. But the shoe was too small and she couldn't fit her big toe in. Her mother handed her a sharp knife and said, "Slice off that toe. Once you're Queen, you won't need to bother with walking." The girl hacked off her toe and pushed her foot into the slipper. She gritted her teeth against the terrible pain and went back to the Prince. Seeing her foot in the golden slipper, the Prince accepted her as his bride and rode off with her on his horse. But their way took them past Ashputtel's mother's grave, and there were the two doves perched in the tree calling,

"Rookity-coo, Rookity-coo!
There's red blood in the golden shoe.
She chopped her toe, it was too wide,
That girl is not your rightful bride."

The Prince looked at her foot and saw the blood oozing out like a clue. He yanked round his horse and galloped straight back to the house and said she was the wrong girl and that the other sister must try on the shoe. So the second sister rushed up to her bedroom and managed to squeeze her toes into the shoe, but her heel wouldn't fit. Her mother handed her the knife and said, "Carve a good slice off your heel. You won't be walking anywhere when you're Queen." The girl chopped off a bit of her heel

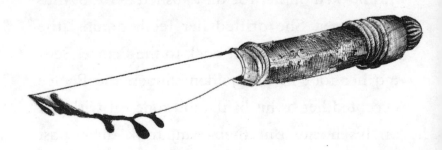

and forced her foot into the shoe. Then she bit her lip against the appalling pain and went back to the Prince. He took her as his bride, lifted her on to his horse and rode off. But as they passed the hazel tree by the grave, the doves were perched there and tell-taled out,

"Rookity-coo, Rookity-coo!
There's red blood in the golden shoe.
She chopped her heel, it was too wide,
And she is not your rightful bride."

The Prince looked at the foot and saw the blood blushing on the slipper and staining her white stocking crimson. So turned round his horse and rode the false girl home. "She's not the right one either," he said. "Have you got another daughter?"

"No," said the man. "The only other girl is a grubby little kitchen-maid who my dead wife left behind her. She can't possibly be the bride."

The King's son asked for her to be sent for.

"No!" cried the stepmother. "She's far too dirty. She's not fit to be looked at."

But the Prince insisted and Ashputtel had to

appear. First, she scrubbed her face and her hands quite clean, then went in and curtsied before the Prince. He handed her the golden shoe.

Ashputtel sat down on a stool, took her lovely foot out of the grotesque wooden clog, and slipped on the little slipper. Of course, it fitted her perfectly, and when she stood up and the Prince looked into her face, he recognized her at once. She was the beautiful girl who had danced with him.

"This is my rightful bride!" he said.

The stepmother and the two sisters were thunderstruck and turned ashen-faced with fury; but the Prince put Ashputtel on his horse and rode off with her.

As they passed the hazel tree, the two white doves sang prettily,

"Rookity-coo, Rookity-coo!
A perfect foot in a golden shoe.
Three times has the good Prince tried,
And now he's found his rightful bride."

When they had sung this, they flew down and perched on Ashputtel's shoulders, one on the left,

46

one on the right, and there they stayed.

On Ashputtel's wedding day, the two false sisters came, hoping to suck up to her and have a share in her good fortune. As the bridal procession was entering the church, the elder sister was on the right and the younger on the left; and the two doves flew at them and pecked out one of each of their eyes. And as they were all coming out of the church, the elder sister was on the left and the younger on the right; and the doves swooped again and pecked out their other eyes. And so, because of their cruelty and deceit, they were punished with blindness for the rest of their ugly days.

Sweet Porridge

for Ella

Once upon a different time there was a very good little girl who lived with her mother, but they were so poor they had nothing left to eat. So the little girl went into the forest, where an old woman met her, who knew of her troubles. She gave her a small pot which, when she said, "Cook, little pot, cook!", would cook sweet and nourishing porridge. When she said, "Stop, little pot," it would stop cooking.

The girl took the pot home to her mother and from then on they were no longer hungry and ate good sweet porridge whenever they wanted.

One day, when the little girl had gone out, her mother said, "Cook, little pot, cook." And it cooked away and she ate till she was quite full up. She wanted the pot to stop cooking then, but she didn't know the right words. So it carried on

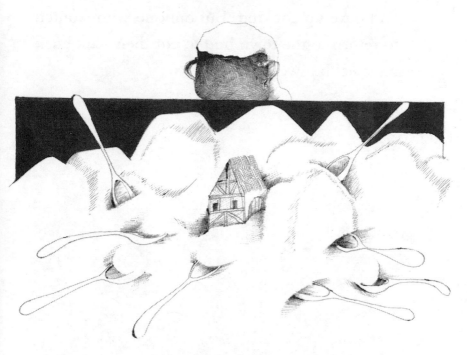

cooking, cooking, until the porridge spilled over
the brim; and it carried on cooking, cooking,
until the kitchen was full, then the whole house,
then the house next door, then the whole street;
and it carried on cooking, cooking, as though it
wanted to satisfy the hunger of the whole world.
It caused the greatest trouble and distress, but no
one knew how to stop it.

At last, when there was only one single house
left, like one spud on a plate, the little girl came
home and said, "Stop, little pot!" And it stopped

and gave up cooking. But anyone who wanted to return to the town had to eat their way back in, street by sweet street.

Iron Hans

Once there was a king whose castle lay next to a great forest which was full of all kinds of wild animals. One day, the King sent out a huntsman to shoot a deer for him; but the huntsman never came back. "Perhaps he's had an accident," said the King, and sent out two more huntsmen to find him. But they didn't return either. On the third day, the King summoned all his huntsmen and ordered, "Scour the whole forest, and don't stop searching till you find all three of them." But none of these huntsmen returned, and not one of the pack of hounds they'd taken with them was ever seen or heard again. From then on no one dared to enter the forest. There it stood, dark and silent and abandoned, with only a lone eagle or hawk flapping over it from time to time.

After many years, a huntsman from another land bowed before the King. He asked permission to stay at his court and volunteered to enter the dangerous forest. The King was reluctant to allow this, saying, "The forest is unlucky. You would do no better than all the others, and I fear that you'd never get out."

But the huntsman replied, "Sire, I will go at my own risk. I am frightened of nothing."

So the huntsman went into the hushed, gloomy forest with his dog. The dog quickly picked up a scent and followed it; but after running a few yards, it was standing in front of a deep pool and could go no further. Suddenly, a naked arm shot out of the water, grabbed the dog and dragged it under quicker than it could bark. When the huntsman saw this, he raced back and got three men to come with pails to bail the water out of the pool. When they had scooped deep enough to see the muddy bottom, they discovered a wild man lying there. His body was the colour of rusty iron and his copper hair hung over his face right down to his knees. They tied him up with ropes and pulled him away to the castle. Everyone there was astonished to see the wild man; but the King had him locked up in an iron cage in the courtyard. It was forbidden, on pain of death, to open the door, and the Queen herself was to mind the key. From then on, everyone could visit the forest safely.

The King had a dear young son. One day, the boy was playing in the courtyard with his golden ball, when it bounced into the cage. He ran up to the prisoner and said, "Can I have my ball back?"

"No," rasped the wild man. "Not unless you open this door for me."

But the boy replied, "No, I won't do that. The King has forbidden it," and he ran off.

The next day he came back and asked for his ball and the wild man croaked, "Open my door." But the boy refused.

On the third day, the King had ridden out to hunt, and the boy came again and said, "I can't open your door even if I wanted to, because I don't have the key."

Then the wild man said, "Your mother guards

54

it under her pillow; you can fetch it from there."
The boy was so keen to have his ball back that
he threw all sense and caution to the winds and
went for the key.

The door was difficult to open and he hurt his
finger doing it. When it was open, the wild man
jumped out, chucked him his golden ball and
hurried away. The boy was scared now, and ran
behind him crying, "Oh, wild man, don't leave,
or else I shall be beaten!" The wild man turned
round, picked him up, put him on his rusty
shoulders and strode rapidly into the forest.

When the King came home, he saw the empty
cage and asked the Queen what had happened.
She knew nothing at all about it and searched
for the key, but it was gone. She called for her
son, but he did not reply. The King sent his servants to hunt for him in the fields and country-
side, but they could not find him. Everyone
could guess what had happened and the whole
court was stooped with grief.

When the wild man was back in his dark, tan-
gly forest, he plucked the boy down from his
shoulders and said to him, "You will not see your

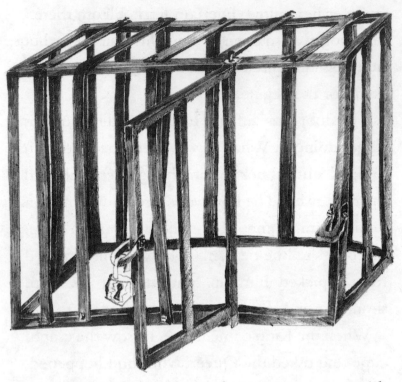

mother and father again, but you can stay with me because you freed me, and I feel something for you. If you do everything I tell you to do, you shall get along fine. I have more gold and treasure than anyone else in the world." Then he made a bed of moss for the boy to sleep on.

The next morning, the wild man took the boy to a spring and said, "Look – this golden spring is as bright and clear as crystal. I want you to stay here and make sure nothing falls into it, or it will get polluted. Every evening I'll come back here to see if you've obeyed my orders." The boy sat down beside the spring. Sometimes he saw a golden fish or a golden snake flash in the water, and he was careful to let nothing fall in. After a bit, his finger began to throb so much that he dipped it into the water without thinking. He quickly whipped it out again, but saw that it had turned golden all over, and he couldn't wipe it off no matter how hard he rubbed.

In the evening, the wild man came back and stared at him. "What has happened to the spring?" he asked.

"Nothing, nothing," said the boy, hiding his finger behind his back.

But the wild man said, "You have dipped your finger into the water. I'll let you off this time, but make sure you don't let anything touch the spring again."

At daybreak next morning, the boy was already sitting by the spring. His finger started to hurt him again. He rubbed it on his head and, by bad luck, a single hair floated down into the spring. He pulled it out quickly, but it was completely golden. The wild man returned and he already knew what had gone on. "You have dropped a hair into the spring," he said. "I'll let you watch the spring once more, but if it happens a third time then the spring is polluted and you cannot stay with me any longer."

On the third morning, the boy sat by the spring and didn't move his finger, however sore it got. But the time dragged slowly, and he grew bored and began staring at his own reflection in the water. As he leaned further and further over, trying to stare himself in the eye, his long hair tumbled down from his shoulders into the spring. He pulled himself up quickly, but all the hair on his head was already golden and shone like the sun. You can imagine how terrified the poor boy was! He took out his handkerchief and tied his hair up so that the man wouldn't see it.

But when he came, he already knew what had happened, and said, "Untie your handkerchief." Then the golden hair streamed out, and although the boy tried to make excuses, it was no use. "You have failed the test and you cannot stay here any longer. Go out alone into the world and find out what hardship is like. But because you have a good heart and I mean you well, I will allow you one thing. If you are ever in trouble, come to the forest and shout 'Iron Hans!' and I will come and help you. My powers are great – greater than you know – and I have more gold and silver than I need."

So the Prince left the forest and walked along the highways, byways, high-roads and low-roads, until at last he arrived at a great city. He looked for work there; but as he had learnt no trade, he had no luck. In the end, he went to the palace and asked if they would have him. The courtiers didn't know what job to give him, but they liked him and let him stay. Then the cook employed him, getting him to carry wood and water and sweep out the ashes.

One day, when no one else was to hand, the cook ordered him to carry the food in to the royal table. Because he didn't want his golden hair to be seen, the boy kept on his hat. This had never happened in the King's presence before, and he said, "When you wait at the royal table, you must remove your hat."

"Oh, sire," the boy answered, "I can't. I've got terrible dandruff."

When he heard this, the King sent for the cook and told him off; asking him what he was thinking of to employ such a boy, and telling him to sack him immediately. But the cook felt sorry for the boy and swapped him for the gardener's lad.

So now the boy had to work in the garden, even in rain or snow, planting and watering and digging and hoeing. One summer's day when he was all alone, it was so hot that he took off his hat to get some fresh air on his head. The sunlight winked and flashed on his golden hair, and the glamorous rays came in through the Princess's window. She jumped up to see what it was, spied the boy and called out to him, "Boy! Bring me a bunch of flowers." He quickly pulled on his hat, gathered some wild flowers and tied them together.

As he was carrying them up the steps, the gardener saw him and said, "How can you take the King's daughter such common flowers? Go and pluck the prettiest and rarest you can for her."

"Oh, no," replied the boy. "Wild flowers have the strongest perfume. She'll like these best."

When he got to her room, the Princess said, "Take off your hat. It's rude to keep it on in my presence."

"I can't," he said again. "I have dandruff on my head."

But she snatched his hat and pulled it off; and then his splendid golden hair cascaded down to his shoulders. He tried to run out, but the Princess held him by the arm and gave him a handful of sovereigns.

The boy went away with them, but he didn't care about gold. So he took them to the gardener and said, "Here, these are a present for your kids to play with."

Next day, the Princess called down that he was to bring her a bunch of wild flowers, and when he brought them she grabbed at his hat, but he held on to it firmly with both hands. She gave him another fistful of gold coins, but he didn't want them and gave them to the gardener again as toys for his children. On the third day, things were just the same – she couldn't pull off his hat, and he wouldn't take her gold.

Not long after this, the whole country went to war. The King gathered his troops together, not knowing whether he'd be able to stand up to the enemy army, which was far bigger in number than his own.

Then the gardener's lad said, "I am grown up now and want to fight in this war too. Give me a horse."

The others laughed and said, "Look for one when we've gone. We'll leave one behind in the stable for you."

When they had set off, the lad went to the stable and led out the horse. It was lame in one foot and limped – hobbledy-clop-clop-clip, hobbledy-clop-clop-clip. But he climbed on and faltered away to the dark forest. When he came to the edge, he called out "Iron Hans!" three times, so loudly that his strong voice echoed among all the trees.

Suddenly the wild man appeared and said, "What do you want?"

"I need a good strong horse. I am off to war."

"You shall have it, and you shall have even

more than you ask for." Then the wild man went back into the forest; and it wasn't long before a groom appeared, leading a powerful horse that snorted and pranced and neighed.

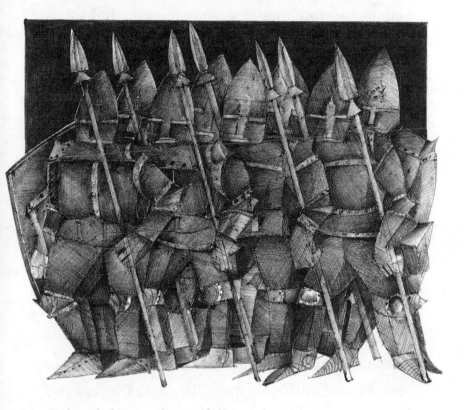

Behind him, there followed a great troop of warriors, all in armour, their swords slicing at the sun. The youth gave his lame horse to the groom, mounted the warhorse and rode off at the head of his soldiers.

When he arrived at the battlefield, many of the King's men had already fallen and the rest were close to defeat. The youth roared up with his troops of iron, charging here and there among the enemy like thunder and lightning, and he struck down everyone who came near him. The enemy began to flee, but he chased them and fought on till there was nobody left. Instead of going back to the King, though, he led his troops the back way to the forest and called for Iron Hans.

"What do you want?"

"Take back your charger and your men in armour and give me back my lame horse." All that he asked for was done, and soon he rode – hobbledy-clop-clop-clip – back home.

When the King returned to the palace, his daughter ran to meet him and congratulated him on winning such a victory. "It wasn't I who won," said her father, "but a strange knight who came to help me with his own soldiers." His daughter wanted to find out who this stranger was, but the King had no idea and said, "He chased after the enemy and I never saw him again."

The Princess asked the gardener where his boy was, but he laughed and said, "He's just limped back on his three-legged nag. The others have been teasing him and shouting out, 'Here comes old hobbledy-nobbledy back again.' They asked him, 'Where have you been then? Kipping under a hedge all this time?' But he said, 'I did better than all of you. Things would have been really bad without me.' And they teased him and laughed at him even more."

The King told his daughter, "I will announce a great feast which will last for three days. You shall throw a golden apple. Perhaps the stranger will show his face."

When he heard about the feast, the young man went back to the forest and called Iron Hans. "What do you want?" Iron Hans asked.

"I want to catch the Princess's golden apple."

"You are practically holding it already," said Iron Hans. "You shall also have a suit of red armour and ride on a magnificent chestnut horse."

When the day of the feast arrived, the young man galloped up to join the other knights, and no one recognized him. The King's daughter stood up and tossed a golden apple to the knights; but he was the only one who caught it, and as soon as he had it in his hand, he thundered away.

On the second day, Iron Hans dressed him as a white knight on a white horse. Again he was the only one who caught the apple and again he galloped away with it. The King grew angry and said, "This behaviour is outrageous. He must come before me and tell me his name." He gave orders that the knight was to be chased if he rode away again, and he was to be threatened with swords if he would not return willingly.

On the third day, Iron Hans gave the young man a suit of black armour and a black horse; and again he caught the apple. But when he spurred away with it, the King's men chased him, and one of them rode close enough to pierce the strange knight's leg with the tip of his sword. He escaped from them despite this, but his horse reared so violently that his helmet fell from his head and they saw his golden hair. They sped back and told all this to the King.

The next day, the Princess asked the gardener

about his boy. "He's working in the garden. What a strange lad he can be. He went to the feast and only got back this morning. Then he showed my children three golden apples he had won."

The King had the gardener's boy brought before him, and the lad came with his hat jammed tight on his head. But the Princess went straight up to him and pulled it off, and then his golden hair fell down to his shoulders and they were all amazed by his beauty.

"Are you the knight who came to the feast every day wearing different colours and who caught the three golden apples?" asked the King.

"Yes," he replied, "and here are the apples." He took them from his pocket and gave them to the King. "If you need more proof, sire, you can see the wound your men gave when they chased me. But I am also the knight who helped you to defeat your enemies."

"If you can perform such heroics, then you are no gardener's boy. Tell me now, who is your father?"

"My father is a rich and powerful king, and I have as much gold as I need."

"I know now," said the King, "that I have much to thank you for. Is there anything I can do to show my gratitude?"

"Yes," he answered, "there certainly is, sire. Give me your daughter's hand in marriage."

When she heard these words, the Princess laughed and said, "Well, he certainly doesn't waste much time, does he! But I knew from his golden hair that he wasn't a gardener's boy!" And she ran up to him and kissed him.

His mother and father came to the wedding and were overjoyed, because they had given up all hope of ever seeing him alive. And as they were all sitting at the wedding-feast, the music suddenly stopped, the doors burst open, and a magnificent king entered in great style. He went up to the young bridegroom, hugged him and said, "I am Iron Hans. I was under a spell that turned me into a wild man but you have set me free! All my gold and treasure will be yours."

The Musicians of Bremen

A man owned a donkey who had worked hard for donkey's years lugging heavy sacks of corn to the mill. But the animal's strength had gone and he was getting more and more unfit for the job. The man was thinking how he could get shut of him and save the expense of feeding him, but the donkey got wind of this and ran away. He clopped off towards Bremen and thought he might try his luck at being a street-musician.

After a while on the road, he came across a hound lying by the roadside, panting away as

though he'd run very fast. So the donkey said, "Hello, old Hound-Dog, what are you gasping like that for?"

The dog answered him, "Arf, I'm not getting any younger and get weaker every day so I can't hunt any more. My master was going to kill me, so I ran off. But how shall I make my living now?"

The donkey said, "I'll tell you what. I'm on my way to Bremen to become a street-musician. Why don't you trot along with me? I'll play the lute and you can bang away at the kettle-drum!" The hound was very taken with this idea and on they went.

Before long, they found a cat slumped by the roadside with a face like three wet Wednesdays.

"Now then, old Lick-Whiskers, what makes you look so miserable?"

The cat answered him, "How else should I look with my problems? Just because I'm getting on and my teeth are worn to stumps and I prefer to sit dreaming by the fire rather than run about after mice, my mistress wants to drown me. So I've run away. But now, who's to advise me what to do and where to go?"

"Come with us to Bremen to be a street-musician. You're well-known for your caterwauling music of the night!"

The cat was impressed with this plan and on the three of them went.

Quite soon our three runaways came to a farm and there on the gate perched a cockerel crowing like crazy.

The donkey called out, "That terrible crowing's going right through us. What on earth's up?"

The cock explained, "I'm forecasting fine weather, because today's wash-day in Heaven and Our Lady wants to dry Baby Jesus's wee shirts. But they've got guests coming here for dinner tomorrow and that callous hard-hearted shrew of a housekeeper has told cook to cook me. My head's for the chop tonight, so I'm having a good old crow while I can."

"Preposterous, Redcomb! Come with us to Bremen instead. You'll be better off there than in a casserole. With that voice of yours and our rhythm, we're going to make music the like of which has never been heard!"

The cock thought this seemed an excellent plan and all four of them went on their way together.

Bremen Town was too far to reach in a day, though, and in the evening they got to a forest where they decided to spend the night. The donkey and the dog lay down under a large tree, the cat settled herself in the branches, and the cock flew right to the top and perched there. Before he went to sleep, he looked to north, south, east and west and thought he spied a quaver of light in the distance. So he called down to his fellow musicians that there must be a house nearby for him to see a light. The donkey said, "Then let's go and find it. The accommodation here's appalling." The hound said that he wouldn't turn up his nose at a plate of bones with some meat on them.

So they set off in the direction of the light, which grew bigger and brighter and more welcoming, until they came to a well-lit house, where a band of robbers were holed up. The donkey, who was the biggest, sneaked up to the window and peeped in.

"What can you see, old Greymule?" asked the cock.

"What can I see! Only a table groaning with wonderful things to eat and drink and a gang of thieves sat round it filling their boots!"

"Those words are music to my ears! That's the kind of thing we're after," said the cock.

"Yes, yes! If only we were inside!"

Then the four famished fugitives put their furry or feathery heads together to decide how to get rid of the robbers. At last they thought of a plan. Old Greymule was to stand on his hind legs with his fore-feet on the window; old Hound-Dog was to jump on the donkey's back; old Lick-Whiskers was to climb on the back of the dog; and lastly Redcomb was to fly up and perch on the head of the cat, like a hat.

When they finally managed all this, the donkey gave a signal, and they launched into their music. The donkey bray-hay-hayed. The cat made mew-mew-music. The hound went Wop-bopawoofwoofbowwowwow. And the cock gave a great big doodly-doodle-do. For an encore, they all crashed into the room through the window, smashing the glass and still boogie-ing. At this horrifying din, the robbers jumped up and thought that a banshee had come screaming into the house. The robbers were so terrified for their lives that they fled freaked into the forest. At this our four friends sat down at the table, well pleased with what was left, and feasted as though they wouldn't see food and drink for a fortnight.

When our four musicians had fin-ished their meal, they put out the  light and found somewhere comfortable to sleep, each according to his needs and nature. The donkey dossed down in the dungheap in the yard. The hound hunched down behind the door. The cat curled up near the ashes on the hearth. And the cock flapped up to roost in the rafters. They were all so tired after their long journey that they soon fell fast asleep.

The robbers were watching the house from a safe distance. When midnight had passed, and they saw that the light was out and all was quiet, their captain said, "Now then, lads. Perhaps we shouldn't have let ourselves be frightened off so easily." He ordered one of his men to creep back up to the house to investigate.

The man found everything as silent and dark as a closed piano-lid, as hushed as drowned bagpipes. He fetched a candle from the kitchen. He thought that the burning red eyes of the cat were glowing coals and stuck his match in them to light it. But the cat didn't appreciate the humour of this and flew in his face, scratching and spitting. The man was terrified out of his wits and ran for the back door but he trod on the dog, who leapt up and bit him savagely on the leg. The robber fled for his life into the yard and was about to leap over the dungheap when he received a whopping kick in the arse from the donkey. All this commotion had wakened the cock, who began to crow on his perch, "Cock-a-doodle-do! Cock-a-doodle-do!"

The robber ran as fast as he could back to his mates and said to the captain, "Oh, my God! There's a horrible witch in the house. I felt her ratty breath and her long claws on my face. Oh, God! There's a man with a blade by the back door who stabbed me in the leg. Oh! There's a hairy monster in the yard who whacked me with a wooden club. God! And to top it all, there's a judge on the roof and he called out, 'That's the crook that'll do! That's the crook that'll do!' So I legged it out of there as fast as I could."

After that, the robbers didn't dare go back to the house. But the four talented members of the Bremen Town Band liked the house so much that they just stayed on. And they're still there.

This story has been told for years. The mouth of the last person to tell this tale still has a warm wet tongue in it – as you can see.

The Lady and the Lion

A merchant was about to go on a long journey, and when he was saying goodbye to his three daughters, he asked each of them what they would like as a present. The eldest asked for pearls, the second asked for diamonds, but the youngest said, "Father, I would like a rose."

Her father said, "It's the middle of winter, but if I can find one, it shall be yours."

When it was time for him to come back home, he'd found pearls and diamonds for the two eldest; but he had searched everywhere without success for a rose. He'd gone into many gardens asking for one, but folk had just laughed and asked did he think roses grew in snow. This upset him, because his youngest girl was his favourite.

He was travelling through a forest. In the middle was a splendid castle and around the castle was a garden. Half of it was in bright summertime and the other half in icy winter. On one side grew the prettiest flowers, but on the other everything was dead and buried in snow. "What a piece of luck!" he said to his servant, and ordered him to pick a rose from the flourishing bush there. But then, as they were riding away, a ferocious lion leapt out, shaking its mane and roaring so loudly that every flower in the garden trembled.

"Anyone who tries to steal my roses will be eaten by me," the lion snarled.

Then the merchant said, "I'd no idea it was your garden. Please forgive me. What can I do to save my life?"

The lion said, "Nothing can save it. Only if you give me what you first meet when you go home. If you agree to do that, then I'll let you live. *And* you can take the rose for your daughter as well."

But the man hesitated and said, "What if it's my youngest daughter? She loves me best and always runs to meet me when I get home."

His servant, though, was scared stiff and said, "It might not be her. It could just as easily be a dog, or a cat."

So the man gave in, took the rose, and promised that the lion should be given whatever he first met when he got home.

When he arrived home and went into his house, his youngest daughter ran up to him and kissed and cuddled him. And she was delighted to see that he'd brought her a rose. But her father started to cry, and said, "My darling child, this rose has cost too much. In exchange for it, I've promised to give you to a savage lion. When he has you, I'm sure he'll rip you to shreds and eat you." He told her everything that had happened and begged her not to go to the lion.

But she comforted him and said, "Dear Father, you must keep your promise. I will go there and make the lion gentle, so that I can come safely home to you."

Next morning, she was shown the way and set off bravely for the forest. The lion, in fact, was an enchanted prince. By day, he and his people were lions; but at night they became humans again. When she arrived, she was treated kindly and taken to the castle. When night fell, the lion turned into a handsome prince and their wedding was held and celebrated with music and dancing. They lived happily together, but he came to her room only when it was dusk and slipped away when morning drew near. After a while, his deep warm voice spoke to her from the darkness, "Your eldest sister is getting married tomorrow and your father is holding a feast. If you would like to go, my lions will escort you there."

"Yes, I'd love to see my father again," she said and set off in the morning with the lions. There was great joy and happiness when she appeared, because everyone thought she'd been torn to pieces and devoured by the wild lion. But she told them her husband was a prince, and how happy she was. She stayed with them till the feast was over, and then returned to the forest.

When her second sister was getting married, she was invited again, and said to her prince, "I don't want to go alone this time. Come with me." But he said it was too dangerous for him, and that he must never be exposed to light. He explained that if, when he was there, so much as a ray of candlelight touched him, he would turn into a dove and have to fly around the world for seven long years.

But the girl pleaded, "Oh, do come with me. I will take special care of you and protect you from all light." So they set off together with their small child.

She chose a room for him there, with walls so thick that no trickle of light could get through. The Prince was to lock himself in there when all the candles were lit for the wedding-feast. But there was a tiny crack in the door that nobody noticed. The wedding was celebrated splendidly, but when the procession came back from church with all its bright, flickering candles, it passed close by his room. A ray as fine as a single hair fell on the Prince; and as soon as it touched him he was transformed. When his wife came to find him, there was only a white dove in the room.

"Now for seven years I must fly around the

globe. But for every seventh step you take, I will drop one white feather. That will show you the way, and if you follow it you can set me free." The dove fluttered out of the door. She followed him. And at every seventh step, a small white feather fell down faithfully and showed her the way, like an arrow.

So she walked and walked and walked through the big wide world – never even resting – and the seven years were almost over. One day, no feather fell; and when she looked up, the dove had disappeared. She thought to herself, "No one human can help me with this." So she climbed up to the sun and said to him, "You shine into every crack, over every mountain; have you seen a white dove flying?"

"No," replied the sun. "I have not. But I'll give you this casket. Open it when you most need help."

She thanked the sun and walked on until it was evening. The moon rose and the girl asked her,

"You shine all night, over all the fields and the forests; have you seen a white dove flying?"

"No," said the moon. "I have not. But I'll give you this egg. Break it when you are desperate."

She thanked the moon and walked on until the night wind began to blow on her. She said to it, "You blow on every tree and under every leaf; have you seen a white dove flying?"

"No," said the night wind. "I have not. But I'll ask the other three winds if they've seen it."

The east and the west winds came and had seen nothing, but the south wind breathed, "I saw the white dove. It has flown to the Red Sea and has become a lion again, because the seven years are now up. The lion is fighting with a dragon, but the dragon is really an enchanted princess."

Then the night wind said to the girl, "Take my advice. Go to the Red Sea. On the right bank you'll see some tall reeds. Count them, break off number eleven, and hit the dragon with it. Then the lion will be able to overpower it and both of them will become human again.

As soon as this happens, run off at once with your prince and travel home by land and sea."

So the poor girl journeyed on and discovered everything just as the night wind had said. She counted the reeds by the sea, snapped off the eleventh, and hit the dragon with it. Then the lion overpowered it and they both became human immediately. But when the Princess, who had been the dragon, was freed from her spell, she grabbed the Prince by the hand and carried him off.

The poor exhausted girl, who had followed and walked so far, sat down and sobbed. But somehow she found her courage and said, "I will still travel as far as the wind blows and as long as the sun and moon shine until I find my love again." And she trudged off along long, long roads until at last she arrived at the castle where the two of them were living together. She found out that there was soon going to be a feast to celebrate their wedding, but she said, "Heaven will help me." Then she opened the casket that the sun had given her. Inside was a dress as dazzling as the sun itself. So she put it on, and went up to the castle. Everyone stared at her in astonishment, even the bride. In fact, the bride liked the dress so much that she wanted it for her wedding dress and asked if it was for sale.

"Not for money or land," the girl answered, "but for flesh and blood."

When the bride asked what she meant, the girl said, "Let me sleep a night in the same room as the bridegroom."

At first the bride wouldn't agree, but she wanted the dress so badly that at last she said yes. But she told her page to give the Prince a sleeping-potion.

When it was night, and the Prince was fast asleep, the girl was taken to his bedchamber. She sat on the bed and said, "I have followed you for seven long years. I have asked the sun and the moon and the four winds for news of you. I have helped you against the dragon. Do you really forget me?" But the Prince slept on and only thought he heard the wind murmuring and sighing in the trees.

When morning came, the girl was removed from his room and had to hand over the golden dress. And because it had all been no use, she wandered sadly into the fields, sat down and cried. While she was sitting there, she remembered the egg which the moon had given to her. So she cracked it open and out came a clucking hen and twelve little chicks made of gold. They ran about chirping and cheeping, then crept under their mother's wings. They were the sweetest sight anyone could see. She stood up and shooed them through the field until the bride looked out of her window. The tiny chicks delighted her so much that she hurried down and asked if they were for sale. "Not for money or land, but for flesh and blood. Let me sleep another night in the bridegroom's chamber."

The bride said yes, but she planned to trick the girl as before. But when the Prince was going to bed, he asked the page what the murmuring and rustling in the night had been. Then the page told him everything: that he'd been forced to give him a sleeping-potion because a strange girl had slept secretly in his room, and that he was supposed to give him another one that night.

The Prince said, "Pour the sleeping-potion away."

At night, the girl was led in again, and when she started to tell him all the sad things that had happened and how faithful to him she had been, he immediately knew the beloved voice of his true wife. He jumped up and cried, "Now I am really released! I have been in a dream, because the strange Princess has bewitched me to make me forget you. But heaven has sent you to me in time, my dear love."

Then they both crept away from the castle, secretly in the dark, because they were afraid of the strange Princess. Together they travelled all the way home where they found their child, who had grown tall and beautiful; and they all lived happily until the very end of their days.

The Fox and the Geese

Then the fox came to a meadow and there sat a flock of fine geese. The fox smirked and said, "My timing is immaculate. There you are all arranged together quite beautifully, like a buffet, so that I can eat you up one after the other." The geese cackled with terror and began to wail and plead piteously for their lives. But the fox would have none of it and said, "Begging is quite useless. There is no mercy to be had. You must die."

At last, one of the geese stepped up and said, "If we poor geese are to lose our healthy young lives, then please allow us one prayer so that we do not die with our sins on our conscience. One final prayer and then we will line up in a row so that you can always pick the plumpest first."

The fox thought, *Yes, that's a reasonable request, and a pious one too.*

"Pray away, geese. I'll wait till you are finished."

So the first goose began a good long prayer, forever saying "Ga! Ga!" and, as she wouldn't stop, the second didn't wait her turn but started praying away as well. "Ga! Ga!" The third and fourth followed her – "Ga, Ga!" – and soon they were all praying and honking and cackling together, holy as heck.

When they have finished their prayers, this story shall be continued further, but at the moment they are still terribly busy praying. Ga! Ga!

Little Red-Cap

There was once a delicious little girl who was loved by everyone who saw her, but most of all by her grandmother, who was always wondering what treat to give the sweet child next. Once she sent her a little red cap which suited her so well that she wouldn't wear anything else and she was known from then on as Little Red-Cap.

One day her mother said, "Little Red-Cap, here are some cakes and a bottle of best wine. Take them to Grandmother. She's been poorly and is still a bit weak and these will do her good. Now hurry up before it gets too hot. And mind how you go, like a good little girl. And don't go wandering off the path in a day-dream, or you'll trip up and smash the wine bottle — because there'll be none left for Grandmother if you do. And when you go into her room, make sure you say a nice 'Good morning' instead of peeping into every corner first!"

Little Red-Cap held her mother's hand and said, "Don't worry, I'll do everything just as you say."

Her grandmother lived out in the wood, a good half an hour's walk from the village, and as soon as Little Red-Cap stepped into the wood, a wolf saw her. Because she didn't know what a wicked animal it was, she wasn't afraid of it.

"Good morning, Little Red-Cap," it said.

"Good morning, wolf."

"And where might you be going so bright and early?"

"To my grandmother's house."

"And what's that you're carrying in your apron?"

"Cakes and wine. We were baking yesterday – and my poor grandmother has been ill. These will build her up again."

"Where does dear Grandmother live, Little Red-Cap?"

"She lives a quarter of an hour's walk from here, under the three big oak trees. Her house has hazel hedges near it. I'm sure you know it."

But the wolf was thinking to itself, *How young and sweet and tender she is. I could eat her. She'll make a plumper mouthful for my chops than the old biddy. If I am wily, though, I can have the pair of them! Two courses!* So the wolf walked beside Little Red-Cap for a bit, and then said, "Look, Little Red-Cap. Open your eyes and see! There are beautiful flowers all around us. And there's wonderful birdsong that you're not even listening to. You just plod straight ahead as though you were going to school – and yet the woods are such fun!"

Little Red-Cap looked around her and when she saw the sunbeams seeming to wink at her among the trees, and when she saw the flung confetti of the flowers leading away from the straight and narrow path, she thought, *Grandmother will be very pleased if I pick her a bunch of lovely fresh flowers. It's still early and I've got plenty of time.*

So she ran from the path, among the trees, picking her flowers, and she kept seeing prettier and prettier flowers which led her deeper and deeper into the wood.

The bad wolf ran fast and straight to the grandmother's house and rapped on the door.

"Who's there?" called out Grandmother.

"Only Little Red-Cap bringing you cake and wine. Open up."

"Lift the latch. I'm too feeble to get out of bed."

So the wolf lifted the latch and the door flew open and without even a word the wolf leapt on the old woman's bed and gobbled her whole. Then it fumbled her nightgown and nightcap over its wolfy fur, crawled into bed and closed the curtains.

All this time, Little Red-Cap had been skipping about among the flowers and when she'd picked as many as her young arms could hold, she remembered her grandmother and hurried off to her house. She was surprised to see that the door was open and as soon as she stepped inside she felt uneasy and said to herself, "Oh, dear, I always look forward to seeing Grandmother, so why do I feel so nervous today?"

"Good morning?" she called, but there was no reply. So she walked over to the bed and drew back the curtains.

Grandmother lay there with her nightcap pulled right down over her face, looking very peculiar indeed.

"Oh, Grandmother, what big ears you have!"

"The better to hear you with, my sweet."

"Oh, Grandmother, what big eyes you have!"

"The better to see you with, my dumpling."

"Oh, Grandmother, what big hands you have!"

"The better to touch you with."

"But Grandmother, what a terrible big mouth you have!"

"The better to eat you."

99

And as soon as the words had left its drooling lips, the wolf made one leap from the bed and wolfed down poor Little Red-Cap. When it had had its fill, the wolf dragged itself on to the bed, and fell fast sleep and started to snore very loudly. The huntsman was just passing the house and thought, *How loudly the old woman is snoring. I'd better see if anything is wrong.* So he went into the house and when he reached the bed he saw the wolf spread out on it like a horrible blanket.

"So you've come here, you vile animal. I've wanted to catch you for a long, long time." The huntsman took aim with his gun and was about to shoot when it flashed through his mind that the wolf might have swallowed the grandmother whole and that she might still be saved. So instead of firing, he got a good pair of scissors and began to snip the warm hairy belly of the sleeping wolf.

After two snips he saw the blood-red colour of the little red cap. Three snips, four snips, five snips more and out jumped Little Red-Cap, crying, "Oh, how frightened I've been! It's so dark inside the wolf!" And then out came her grandmother, hardly breathing, but still alive.

Little Red-Cap rushed outside and quickly fetched some big stones and they filled the wolf's belly with them. When the wolf woke up, it tried to run away, but the stone loaves in its evil gut were too heavy and it dropped down dead.

When this happened, all three were delighted. The huntsman skinned the wolf and strode home with its pelt in his belt. The grandmother ate the cake and drank the wine and soon began to feel like a new woman. And Little Red-Cap promised herself, "Never ever, so long as I live, will I wander off the path into the woods when my mother has warned me not to."

Two Households

"Where are you off to?"

"Off to Walpe."

"You're for Walpe, I'm for Walpe. So, so, together we'll go."

"Got a man? What's his name?"

"Dan."

"Your man's Dan, my man's Dan. You're for Walpe, I'm for Walpe. So, so, together we'll go."

"Got a child? How's she styled?"

"Wild."

"Your child's Wild, my child's Wild. Your man's Dan, my man's Dan. You're for Walpe, I'm for Walpe. So, so, together we'll go."

"Got a cradle? What's the label?"

"Hippodadle."

"Hippodadle cradle, Hippodadle cradle. Your child's Wild, my child's Wild. Your man's Dan, my man's Dan. You're for Walpe, I'm for Walpe. So, so, together we'll go."

"Got a servant? What's his title?"

"Stay-a-Bed Bone-Idle."

"Your servant Stay-a-Bed Bone-Idle, my servant Stay-a-Bed Bone-Idle. Hippodadle cradle, Hippodadle cradle. Your child's Wild, my child's Wild. Your man's Dan, my man's Dan. You're for Walpe, I'm for Walpe. So, so, together we'll go."

The Hare and the Hedgehog

This tale, my splendid young reader, may seem to you to be false, but it really is true, because I heard it from my grandmother, and when she told it she always said, "It must be true, my dear, or else no one could tell it to you." Here goes.

One Sunday morning around harvest time, just as the wheat was blooming, the sun shining, the breeze blowing, the larks singing, the bees buzzing, the folk off to church in their best clobber, everything that lived was happy and the hedgehog was happy too.

The hedgehog was stood by his own front door, arms akimbo, relishing the morning and singing a song to himself half-aloud. It was no better or worse a song than the songs which hedgehogs usually sing on a sabbath morning. His wife was inside, washing and drying the children, and he suddenly fancied taking a stroll in the field to see how his turnips were getting on. The turnips grew beside the hedgehog's house and the hedgehog family were in the habit of eating them – because of this he thought of them as his. The hedgehog clicked shut his front door and set off for the field.

He hadn't gone very far and was just turning round that big bush which grows outside the field, when he noticed the hare. The hare was out and about on a similar enterprise to visit his cabbages. The hedgehog called a neighbourly good morning. But the hare, a distinguished gentleman in his own way, was hoity-toity and gave the hedgehog a snooty look. He didn't say good morning back, but spoke in a very con-temptuous manner, "What brings you scamper-ing about in the field so early in the morning?"

"I'm taking a walk," said the hedgehog.

"A walk!" said the hare with a haughty sneer. "Surely you can think of a more suitable use for those legs of yours."

These words made the hedgehog bristle and quiver with rage. He couldn't stand any mention of his legs, which are naturally crooked.

The hedgehog said, "You seem to think you can do more with your legs that I can with mine."

"That's exactly what I think."

"That can soon be put to the test. I'll bet that if we run a race, I shall beat you."

"That's preposterous! With those hedgehoggy legs? Well, I'm perfectly willing if you have such a ridiculous fancy for it. What shall we wager?"

"A golden sovereign and a bottle of brandy."

"Done. Shake hands on it. We might as well do it at once."

But the hedgehog said, "Nay, nay, there's no rush. I'm going home for some breakfast. I'll be back at this very spot in half an hour."

The hare was quite satisfied with this, so the hedgehog set off home. On his way he thought to himself, *The hare is betting on his long legs, but I'll get the better of him. He may be an important gentleman, but he's a cocky creature and he'll pay for his cutting words.*

When the hedgehog got back home, he called to his wife, "Wife, dress yourself quickly. You've got to come up to the field with me."

"What's going on?" said his wife.

"I've made a bet with the hare for a gold sovereign and a bottle of brandy, and we have to race each other. You must be there."

But his wife was aghast and appalled. "Husband, are you not right in the head? What are you thinking of, running a race with the hare?"

The hedgehog snapped, "Hold your tongue, woman. That's my affair. Don't try to discuss things which are matters for men. Now get yourself dressed and follow me."

What else was the lawful wife of a hedgehog to do? She had to obey him, like it or like it not.

So they set off together and the hedgehog told his wife, "Pay attention to what I'm saying. The long field will be our racecourse. I'll run in one furrow and the hare in t'other. We'll start from the top. You position yourself at the bottom of the furrow. When the hare arrives at the end of furrow next to you, just shout out, 'I'm here already!'"

They reached the field. The hedgehog showed his wife her place, then walked up to meet the hare.

"Shall we start then?" drawled the hare.

"Ready when you are," piped the hedgehog.

"Then let's go."

They each got in their furrow. The hare counted "Once. Twice. Thrice and away!" and flew off at the speed of arrogance down the field. But the hedgehog only trotted three steps, then crouched down, quiet and sleekit in his furrow.

As soon as the hare arrived full pelt at the bottom of the field, the hedgehog's wife was already there saying, "I'm here already!"

The hare was flabbergasted. He thought it really was the hedgehog because the wife was the spit of her spouse. But he thought, *This hasn't been done fairly*. He said, "We must run again. Let us do it again." And a second time he whooshed off like a whirlwind.

But the hedgehog's wife stayed modestly in her place and when the hare reached the other end of the field, there was the hedgehog himself crying out, "I'm here already!" The hare was hopping with fury, and kept saying, "Again! Again! We must run it again!"

The hedgehog said, "Fine. I'm happy to run as often as you like."

The hare ran another seventy-three times. Each time, the hedgehog tricked him. Every time the hare reached one end of the field, the hedgehog or his wife said, "I'm here already." But at the seventy-fourth time, the hare couldn't make it to the end. He collapsed in the middle of the field and a finishing-tape of blood streamed from his mouth. The hare was dead. The hedgehog ran up and removed the gold sovereign which he had won and the bottle of brandy from the late hare. He called his wife out of her furrow and the pair of them swaggered home on their eight legs in great delight. If they're not dead, they're still alive.

The moral of this story is, firstly, that no matter how grand a person might be, they should not poke fun at anyone beneath themselves — not even a hedgehog. Secondly, it shows that a chap should marry someone in his own position, who looks just like he looks himself. Whoever is a hedgehog must be jolly sure that his wife is a hedgehog as well. And so on. And so forth.

Clever Hans

Hans's mother said, "Where are you off to Hans?"

Hans said, "To see Gretel."

"Behave well, Hans."

"Oh, I'll behave well. Goodbye, Mother."

"Goodbye, Hans."

Hans goes to Gretel. "Good day, Gretel."

"Good day, Hans. What have your brought that's good?"

"I've brought nowt. I want to have something given me." Gretel presents Hans with a needle. "Goodbye, Gretel."

"Goodbye, Hans."

Hans takes the needle, sticks it into a hay cart, follows the cart home.

"Good evening, Mother."

"Good evening, Hans. Where have you been?"

"With Gretel."

"What did Gretel give you?"

"Gave me a needle."

"Where is the needle, Hans?"

"Stuck in the hay cart."

"That was badly done, Hans. You should have stuck the needle in your sleeve."

"Not to worry. I'll do better next time."

"Where are you off to, Hans?"

"To Gretel, Mother."

"Behave well, Hans."

"Oh, I'll behave well. Goodbye, Mother."

"Goodbye, Hans."

Hans goes to Gretel. "Good day, Gretel."

"Good day, Hans. What have your brought that's good?"

"I've brought nowt. I want to have something given to me." Gretel presents Hans with a knife. "Goodbye, Gretel."

"Goodbye, Hans."

Hans takes the knife, sticks it in his sleeve and goes home.

"Good evening, Hans. Where have you been?"

"With Gretel."

"What did you take her?"

"Took nowt. Got given something."

"What did Gretel give you?"

"Gave me a knife."

"Where is the knife, Hans?"

"Stuck in my sleeve."

"That was badly done, Hans. You should have put the knife in your pocket."

"Not to worry. I'll do better next time."

"Where are you off to, Hans?"

"To Gretel, Mother."

"Behave well, Hans."

"Oh, I'll behave well. Goodbye, Mother."

"Goodbye, Hans."

Hans goes to Gretel. "Good day, Gretel."

"Good day, Hans. What good thing have you brought?"

"I've brought nowt. I want something given

me." Gretel presents Hans with a young goat.

Hans takes the goat, ties its legs and stuffs it in his pocket. When he gets it home it has suffocated.

"Good evening, Mother."

"Good evening, Hans. Where have you been?"

"With Gretel."

"What did you take her?"

"Took nowt. Got given something."

"What did Gretel give you?"

"She gave me a goat."

"Where is the goat, Hans?"

"Put it in my pocket."

"That was badly done, Hans. You should have put a rope round the goat's neck."

"Not to worry. Do better next time."

"Where are you off to, Hans?"

"To Gretel, Mother."

"Behave well, Hans."

"Oh, I'll behave well. Goodbye, Mother."

"Goodbye, Hans."

Hans goes to Gretel. "Good day, Gretel."

"Good day, Hans. What good thing have you brought me?"

"I've brought nowt. I want something given me." Gretel presents Hans with a piece of bacon. "Goodbye, Gretel."

"Goodbye, Hans."

Hans takes the bacon, ties it to a rope and drags it away behind him. The dogs come sniffing and scoff the bacon. When he gets home he has the rope in his hand with nothing at the end of it.

"Good evening, Mother."

"Good evening, Hans. Where have you been?"

"With Gretel."

"What did you take her?"

"Took nowt. Got given something."

"What did Gretel give you?"

"Gave me a bit of bacon."

"Where is the bacon, Hans?"

"I tied it to a rope, pulled it home. Dogs had it."

"That was badly done, Hans. You should have carried the bacon on your head."

"Not to worry. Do better next time."

"Where are you off to, Hans?"

"To Gretel, Mother."

"Behave well, Hans."

"Oh, I'll behave well. Goodbye, Mother."

"Goodbye, Hans."

Hans goes to Gretel. "Good day, Gretel."

"Good day, Hans. What have you brought that's good?"

"I've brought nowt. I want something given me."

Gretel presents Hans with a calf.

"Goodbye, Gretel."

"Goodbye, Hans."

Hans takes the calf and hoists it on to his head. The calf gives his face a right kicking.

"Good evening, Mother."

"Good evening, Hans. Where have you been?"

"With Gretel."

"What did you take her?"

"Took nowt. Got given something."

"What did Gretel give you?"

"A calf."

"Where is the calf, Hans?"

"I put it on my head and it kicked my face in."

"That was badly done, Hans. You should have led the calf and put it in the stable."

"Not to worry. Do better next time."

"Where are you off to, Hans?"

"To Gretel, Mother."

"Behave well, Hans."

"Oh, I'll behave well. Goodbye, Mother."

"Goodbye, Hans."

Hans goes to Gretel. "Good day, Gretel."

"Good day, Hans. What good thing have you brought?"

"I've brought nowt. I want something given me."

Gretel says to Hans, "I will come with you."

Hans takes Gretel, ties her with a rope, leads her to the stable and locks her up. Then Hans goes to his mother.

"Good evening, Mother."

"Good evening, Hans. Where have you been?"

"With Gretel."

"What did you take her?"

"I took her nowt."

"What did Gretel give you then?"

"She gave me nowt. She came back with me."

"Where have you left Gretel?"

"I led her by the rope, tied her up in the stable, and scattered a bit of straw for her."

"That was very badly done, Hans. You should have cast warm eyes on her."

"Not to worry. Will do better."

Hans marched into the stable, scooped and gouged and cut out all the calves' and sheep's eyes and threw them in Gretel's face. At this, she became very angry, tore herself loose and fled from the stable. Gretel was finished with Hans.

Snow White

In the cold heart of winter, when snow fell as though the white sky had been ripped into a million pieces, a queen sat by a window sewing. The frame of the window was made of black ebony. And as the Queen sewed and gazed out at the snow, she pricked her finger with the needle and three drops of blood fell upon the snow. The red looked so pretty against the white that the Queen suddenly thought to herself, *I wish I could have a child as white as the snow, as red as blood and as black as the wood on the window frame.*

Soon after that, she had a little daughter who was born as white as snow, with blood-red lips and hair which gleamed like black ebony. She was called Snow White and when she gave the first cry of birth, the Queen died.

After a year had gone by, the King married

again. His new wife was a beautiful woman, but she was proud and vain and couldn't stand the thought of anyone else being more beautiful. She owned a wonderful mirror and when she stood before it, admiring her reflection, she said,

"Mirror, mirror on the wall,
Who in this land is the fairest of all?"

The mirror replied:

"You are, Queen. Fairest of all."

Then she was pleased because she knew the mirror always told the truth.

But Snow White was growing up, and becoming more and more beautiful. And when she was seven years old she was as lovely as the day and ever, and more beautiful than the Queen herself.

One day, the Queen asked her mirror,

"Mirror, mirror on the wall,
Who in this land is fairest of all?"

And the mirror answered,

"Queen, you are beautiful, day and night,
But even more lovely is little Snow White."

Then the Queen got a shock, and turned yellow and green with poisonous envy. From that moment, whenever she looked at Snow White, her heart turned sour in her breast, she hated her so much. Envy and pride crept and coiled round her heart like ugly weeds, so that she could get no peace night or day. At last she called a huntsman and said, "Take the girl into the forest. I want her out of my sight. Kill her – and bring me back her liver and lungs to prove it."

The huntsman did what the Queen ordered and took Snow White away – but when he pulled out his knife to stab her innocent heart, Snow White cried and said, "Please, dear huntsman, spare my life! I will run away into the wild wood and never come back!"

And as she was so beautiful, the huntsman took pity on her and said, "Poor child. Run away then." *The wild beasts will eat you anyway, he thought*; but he felt as though a cruel hand had stopped squeezing his heart because he wasn't going to kill her. A young boar ran by and he slaughtered it, hacked out its liver and lungs and took them dripping to the Queen to prove that the girl was dead. The cook had to salt, slice and serve them and the bad Queen devoured them and thought she'd eaten Snow White's lungs and liver.

But Snow White was alone in the forest and terrified. She began to run, over stones as sharp as envy, through thorns as spiteful as long fingernails. Wild beasts ran past her, but did not harm her. She ran as long as her feet could carry her, until it was almost evening. It was then that she saw a little cottage and went into it to rest. Everything in the cottage was small, but neater and cleaner than prose can tell. There was a table with a white tablecloth and seven little plates, each with its own spoon. There were seven little knives and forks and seven little tankards. Against the wall were seven little beds side by side, each one covered with a snow-white eiderdown.

Snow White was so hungry and thirsty that she ate a mouthful of bread and vegetables from each plate and sipped a swallow of wine from each mug. She was so sleepy that she lay down on one of the little beds, but none of them suited her. One was too long, one too short, one too soft, one too hard, one too lumpy, one too smooth. But the seventh was perfect, so she snuggled down in it, said a prayer, and drifted off to sleep.

When it was dark, the owners of the cottage came back. They were seven dwarfs who worked in the mountains digging for copper and gold. They put seven matches to seven candles to fill the cottage with light and saw at once that someone had been there.

The first said, "Who's been sitting in my chair?"

The second, "Who's been eating off my plate?"

The third, "Who's had some of my bread?"

The fourth, "Who's been biting my vegetables?"

The fifth, "Who's been prodding with my fork?"

The sixth, "Who's been cutting with my knife?"

Then the first one looked about and saw there was a little hollow on his bed, and he said, "Who's been lying on my bed?"

The others crowded round and each one shouted out, "Somebody's been getting into my bed too!" But the seventh dwarf found Snow White lying asleep in his bed and he called the others. They cried out with amazement and fetched their seven little candles and let the warm light fall on Snow White. "Oh goodness! Oh mercy!" they said. "What a beautiful child."

They were so pleased that they let her sleep peacefully on. The seventh dwarf bunked in with his companions, one hour with each dwarf, and so spent the night, and was happy to do so.

When morning came, Snow White woke up and was frightened when she saw the seven dwarfs. But they were friendly and asked her her name. "My name is Snow White," she replied.

"How have you come to our house?" asked the dwarfs.

She told them that her stepmother had ordered her to be killed, but that the huntsman had taken pity on her and she had run through the forest for a whole day until she arrived at their little cottage.

The dwarfs said, "If you will look after our house, make the beds, set the table, keep everything neat and tidy, cook, wash, sew, knit and mend, you can live here with us and you shall have everything you need."

"With all my heart!" said Snow White, and she stayed with the seven dwarfs. She kept the house exactly as they wanted. In the mornings they went off to the mountain to dig and delve for copper and gold. In the evenings they returned and then their supper had to be on the table. The young girl was alone all day, so the dwarfs warned her to be careful. "Beware of your stepmother. She will soon find out you are here. Don't let anyone into the house."

But the Queen believed that she'd eaten the lungs Snow White breathed with, and that once again she was more beautiful than anyone. She swanned to her mirror and said,

"Mirror, mirror on the wall,
Who in this land is fairest of all?"

And the mirror replied,

"Queen, you're the fairest I can see.
But deep in the wood where seven dwarfs
dwell,
Snow White is still alive and well,
And you are not so fair as she."

Then the Queen was appalled because she knew that the mirror never lied and that the huntsman had tricked her. Her envious heart gnawed away inside her and her wicked mind thought and thought how she might kill Snow White — for so long as she wasn't the fairest in the land she could have no peace.

At last she thought of a plan. She stained her face and dressed up like an old pedlar-woman, so that not even her own mirror would have known her. In this disguise she made her way to the house of the seven dwarfs. She knocked at the door and sang out, "Pretty things for sale, very cheap, very cheap."

Snow White looked out of the window and called back, "Good day, pedlar-woman, what are you selling today?"

"Beautiful things, pretty things, fair things, skirt-laces of all colours."

The sly Queen pulled out a lace of bright-coloured silk.

I can let this friendly old woman in, thought Snow White, and she unlocked the door and bought the fine laces.

But the old woman said, "Child, what a sight you are! Come here and let the old pedlar-woman lace you up properly for once!"

Snow White didn't suspect a thing and stood before her and let herself be laced with the new laces. But the old woman laced so quickly and viciously and tightly that Snow White lost her breath and fell down as if she were dead. "Now I am the most beautiful," crowed the Queen and hurried away.

Soon afterwards, when evening fell, the seven dwarfs came home – but how distressed they were to see their dear little Snow White lying on the ground. They lifted her up and, when they saw she was laced too tightly, they cut the laces. Then Snow White started to breathe a little and after a while came back to life. When the dwarfs heard what had happened, they said, "The old pedlar-woman was really the evil Queen. Be more careful. Let nobody in when we are not here."

The Queen ran home and went straight to her mirror:

"Mirror, mirror on the wall
Who in this land is fairest of all?"

And the mirror replied as before,

"Deep in the wood where seven dwarfs dwell,
Snow White is still alive and well.
Although you're the fairest I can see,
Queen, you are not so fair as she."

When she heard the mirror's words, the Queen's blood flooded her heart with fear, for she knew it was true that Snow White was alive. But she said, "Now I will think of something that will really rid me of you forever." And by the help of witchcraft, which she had studied, she made a poisonous comb. Then she disguised herself in the shape of another old woman, made her malevolent way to the house of the seven dwarfs and knocked at the door.

"Good things for sale, cheap, cheap."

Snow White looked out and said, "Go away, please. I can't let anyone in."

"You can at least look," said the old woman, and held out the poisonous comb.

Snow White admired the comb so much that she let herself be fooled and opened the door. When they had agreed a price, the old woman said, "Now I'll comb your ebony hair properly for once."

Poor Snow White had no suspicion and let the old woman do as she wished. But no sooner had the crone put the comb in the girl's hair than the poison took effect and Snow White fell down senseless.

"You prize beauty," spat the wicked woman. "You are nothing now." And she slid away.

As luck would have it, it was nearly evening, when the seven dwarfs were due home. When they saw Snow White left for dead on the ground they immediately suspected the step-mother, and they looked and found the poisonous comb. They took it out and Snow White soon came to herself and told them what had happened. Then they warned her yet again to be on her guard and to open the door to no one.

The Queen was back home with her mirror:

"Mirror, mirror on the wall,
Who in this land is fairest of all?"

The mirror answered as before,

"Queen, you're the fairest I can see.
But deep in the wood where seven dwarfs dwell
Snow White is still alive and well
And no one's as beautiful as she."

When she heard the mirror speak like this, the Queen trembled and shook with rage and swore, "Snow White shall die, even if it costs me my life."

She went into a quiet, secret, lonely room where no one ever came, and there she made a very poisonous apple. On the outside it looked pretty – crisp and white with a blood-red cheek, so that everyone who saw it longed for it – but whoever ate a piece of it would die.

Then she painted her face, disguised herself as a farmer's wife, and went for the third time to the house of the seven dwarfs. She banged her fist on the door.

Snow White put her head out of the window and said, "I can't let anyone in. The seven dwarfs have forbidden me."

"It's all the same, to me, pet. I'll soon get rid of my juicy apples. Here — you can have one."

"No, I dare not take anything."

"Are you afraid it might be poisoned? Look, I'll cut the apple in two pieces, you eat the red cheek and I will eat the white."

But the apple was so cunningly made that only the red cheek was poisoned. Snow White longed for the tantalizing fruit and when she saw the farmer's wife sink her teeth into it, she couldn't resist any more and stretched out her hand and took the poisonous half. But as soon as she'd taken a bite into her mouth, she fell down dead.

The Queen gazed at her long and hard with a dreadful look and laughed horribly and said,

"Snow White,
Blood Red,
Black as Coffin Wood —
This time the seven dwarfs

Will find you dead for good."

She ran home quickly, quickly. She rushed rasping to her mirror. She panted out the words again,

"Mirror, mirror, on the wall,
Who in this land is fairest of all?"

And the mirror answered at last,

"Oh, Queen, in this land you are fairest of all."

When the dwarfs came home in the evening, they found Snow White lying on the ground. She breathed no longer and was dead. They lifted her up and looked for anything poisonous, unlaced her, combed her hair, washed her in water and wine, but it was all useless. The girl was dead and stayed dead. So they laid her upon a bier and the seven of them sat round it and for three whole days they wept for Snow White.

Then they were going to bury her, but she still looked so vividly alive with her pretty red cheeks. They said, "We cannot put her in the cold dark earth." So they had a coffin of glass made, so that she could be seen from all sides. They laid her in it and put her name on it in gold letters and that she was daughter of a king. They carried the coffin up to the mountain and one of them always guarded it. Birds came, too, to weep for Snow White. First an owl, then a raven and lastly a dove.

And now Snow White lay for a very long time in her glass coffin as though she were only sleeping; still as white as snow, as red as blood, and with hair as black as ebony.

It happened, though, that a king's son came to the forest and went to the dwarfs' house to spend the night. He saw the coffin glinting like a mirror on the mountain, and he climbed up and saw Snow White inside it and read what was written there in letters of gold. He said to the dwarfs, "Let me have the coffin. I will give you anything you name for it."

But the dwarfs answered that they wouldn't part with it for all the treasure in the world.

Then the King's son said, "Let me have it as a gift. My heart cannot beat without seeing Snow White. I will honour and cherish her above all else in this world." Because he spoke like this, the dwarfs felt for him and gave him the coffin.

The King's son had it carried away on his servants' shoulders. As they were doing this, they tripped over some tree roots, and with the jolt the piece of poisoned apple which Snow White had swallowed came out of her throat. She opened her eyes, lifted the coffin lid and sat up, as warm and alive as love.

"Heaven's! Where am I?" she asked.

The King's son was shining like an apple with delight and said, "You are with me." He told her what had happened and said, "I love you more than my heart can hold. Come with me to my father's palace. Be my wife."

Snow White was willing and did go with him, and their wedding was held with great show and splendour. Snow White's wicked stepmother was invited to the festivities. When she was dressed in her best jewels and finery, she danced to the mirror and queried,

"Mirror, mirror, on the wall,
Who in this land is fairest of all?"

The mirror answered,

"You are the old Queen. That much is true.
But the new young Queen is fairer than you."

Then the wicked woman cursed and swore and was so demented, so wretched, so distraught, that she could hardly think. At first, she wouldn't go to the feast, but she had no peace, and had to clap eyes on the young Queen. So she went. And when she walked in she saw that it was Snow White and was unable to move with fear and rage. She stood like a statue of hate. But iron dancing shoes were already heating in the fire. They were brought in with tongs and set before her. Then she was forced to put on the red-hot shoes and she was made to dance, dance, until she dropped down dead.

Brother Scamp

Before your time there was a great war and when it was over many soldiers were discharged. One of these was Brother Scamp. He was given one loaf of ammunition-bread and four shillings and sent on his way. St Peter, however, had disguised himself as a beggar and was sitting by the roadside. When Brother Scamp came along, he begged for charity.

Brother Scamp answered him, "Dear beggar, what am I to give you? I've been a soldier, but on my dismissal I was given only this loaf of ammunition-bread and four shillings. Once they've gone, I shall have to go begging myself. Even so, I'll give you something." Then Brother Scamp divided his loaf into four parts, gave one to St Peter, and tossed him a shilling as well.

The apostle thanked him and hurried on his way; but further along the road he sat down again disguised as a different beggar. When Brother Scamp came along, he begged for a gift as before. Brother Scamp spoke as he had earlier and again gave him a piece of bread and a shilling. St Peter thanked him and went on, but for the third time squatted down in Brother

Scamp's path disguised as a beggar. He held out his hand again. Brother Scamp said the same thing again and once more gave him a quarter of bread and a shilling. St Peter thanked him.

Brother Scamp, with only one shilling and the last morsel of bread left, went on to an inn where he ate the bread and ordered a shilling's worth of ale. When he had finished, he hit the road and soon met St Peter, this time kitted-out as a discharged soldier like himself.

"Good day, comrade. Can you spare a bit of bread and a shilling for some beer?"

"You can't spare what you've not got," said Brother Scamp. "I've been discharged and all the army gave me was a loaf of ammunition-bread and four shillings. I met three beggars on the road and I gave each of them a quarter of bread and a shilling. I ate the last quarter of bread at an inn and spent the last shilling on ale. So now my pockets are empty. If you're in the same boat, then why don't we go begging together?"

St Peter said, "There's no need to go begging. I know a bit about healing. I'll soon make as much as I need from that."

"Well," said Brother Scamp, "I know less than nothing about all that, so I'd better go begging on my own."

"Just come along with me," said St Peter, "and if I make any money at it you can have half."

"Fair enough," said Brother Scamp, and the two soldiers marched off together.

They soon came to a peasant's house, from which they heard loud weeping and cries of lamentation. They went in. A man lay there, very sick and at death's door, and his poor wife was wailing her lungs out.

"Stop your weeping and wailing," said St Peter, "I will make this man well again." He took some ointment from his pocket and healed the man quicker than an angel's wing. The man jumped up in the best of health.

The husband and wife were overjoyed and said, "How can we thank you? What can we give you to repay you?" But St Peter wouldn't accept any reward; and the more the peasant folk offered, the more he refused.

Brother Scamp nudged St Peter, "Take something, for God's sake. We need it!"

Finally, the woman brought in a lamb and told St Peter that he really must take it. But St Peter didn't want to.

Then Brother Scamp gave him a poke and hissed, "Take it, take it. We need it!"

At last St Peter said, "All right I'll accept it. But I won't carry it. If you want it so much, then you can carry it."

"Fair enough," said Brother Scamp, and hoisted the lamb on to his shoulder.

They hiked on together and came to a forest. By this time, Brother Scamp was beginning to find the lamb very heavy, and he was starving as well. So he said to his companion, "Look, this is a good enough spot. Let's stop and cook the lamb and eat it."

"If you like," said St Peter. "But I can't cook. If you want to cook, there's a pot. I shall go for a walk until it's ready. But you mustn't start eating till I get back. I will be here at the right time."

"Off you pop," said Brother Scamp. "I'm a nifty hand at cooking. Just leave everything to me."

When St Peter had gone, Brother Scamp
butchered the lamb, lit the fire, threw the meat
into the pot and cooked it. After a while, the
meat was ready, but St Peter still hadn't
returned. Brother Scamp removed the meat
from the pot, cut it up, and found the heart.
That's reckoned to be the best part, he thought to
himself. He tasted a wee bit, then nibbled a little
bit more, and a little bit more, and soon he had
scoffed not just part of the heart, but the whole
heart.

Eventually, St Peter came back and said, "You can eat the whole lamb yourself. Just give me the heart."

Brother Scamp took a knife and fork and pretended to look for the heart. He poked and prodded anxiously among the flesh and finally gave up. "There isn't any heart," he said.

"How can that be?" said St Peter.

"Search me," said Brother Scamp. "But hang on a minute! What idiots we are! Everyone knows that a lamb hasn't got a heart."

"Let's go then. If there's no heart, I don't want any lamb. You can have it all for yourself."

"What I can't manage now, I'll take away in my knapsack," said Brother Scamp. He polished off half the lamb and packed the leftovers into his knapsack.

They went on their way and after a while St Peter arranged for a wide stream of water to block their path. They had to cross it somehow and St Peter said, "You go first."

But Brother Scamp said, "No, after you, comrade." And he thought, *If the water turns out to be too deep for him, I can stay behind.*

St Peter waded across and the water only came up to his knees. So Brother Scamp followed him, but the water got deeper and deeper until it was up to his neck. Then he shouted, "Brother! Help me!"

"Admit you ate the lamb's heart!"

"No! I didn't eat it!"

The water grew even deeper until it was up to his mouth. Brother Scamp cried out again, "Brother! Help me!"

"Confess! Say you ate the lamb's heart!"

"No! I didn't eat it!"

But St Peter would not let the man drown, so he made the water subside and helped him across.

They took to the road again and came to a kingdom where they heard that the King's daughter was ill and at death's door. The soldier turned to St Peter, "Now then, comrade! This is right up our street. If we can cure her, we'll be set up for life!"

St Peter agreed, but walked too slowly for Brother Scamp's liking.

"Get a move on, Brother. We want to get there

before it's too late. Come on!" But the more Brother Scamp pushed and shoved, the slower St Peter went; and before long they heard that the Princess had died.

"I knew this would happen!" said Brother Scamp. "This is what comes of your dawdling along."

"Hold your tongue," said St Peter. "I don't just heal sick people. I can make dead people live again."

"Well, if that's the case," said Brother Scamp, "make sure we get a decent reward. Ask for half the kingdom, at least."

They went to the royal palace, where everyone was distraught with grief. St Peter went straight to the King and swore to him that he would bring his daughter back to life. He was taken to her room and said, "Bring me a cauldron of water." They brought the water and he told everyone to leave the room except for Brother Scamp. St Peter cut off the dead girl's arms and legs and tossed them into the water. He made a fire under the cauldron and boiled them. When all the flesh had fallen off, he took the clean white bones out of the water, placed them on a table, and arranged them in the correct order. When he'd done all this to his satisfaction, he stepped forward and said three times, "In the name of the Holy Trinity, dead Princess, stand up and live again."

At his third chant, the girl stood up, warm and well and lovely. The King was shaking with joy and gratitude and said to St Peter, "Name your reward. Even if you ask for half my kingdom you shall have it."

But St Peter replied, "I want nothing."

Oh, you cabbage-head! thought Brother Scamp. He nudged his partner in the ribs and muttered, "Don't be so daft. You might not want a reward, but I do."

St Peter still wanted nothing, but the King saw that the other man felt quite the opposite and ordered his treasurer to fill Brother Scamp's knapsack with gold.

Again they went on their way. When they came to a forest, St Peter said to Brother Scamp, "Now we'll share out the gold."

"Fair enough."

St Peter divided the gold into three parts. Brother Scamp thought to himself, *What rubbish has old cauliflower-brains got into his head now? Why split the gold into three when there's only two of us?*

St Peter spoke, "I've split the gold perfectly. One part for me, one for you, and one for who-ever ate the lamb's heart."

"That was me!" said Brother Scamp, and scooped up the gold swift as a double-wink. "Word of honour."

"How is that possible," said St Peter, "when we know that a lamb has no heart?"

"What are you on about, Brother? Everyone knows a lamb has a heart, same as any other animal. Why shouldn't it?"

"Very well," said St Peter, "keep the gold for yourself. I have had enough of your company and I'm going on by myself."

"If that's what you want then fair enough, Brother," the soldier said. "Goodbye."

So St Peter took a different road and Brother Scamp thought, *I'm glad to see the back of him. What a weird bloke he turned out to be.* He now had

plenty of money, but he didn't know how to use it sensibly. He squandered some, gave some away, spent the change, and pretty soon he was skint yet again.

He came to a land where he was told that the King's daughter had died. He thought to himself, *Hang about! There might be something in this for me. I'll bring her back to life and make sure I get a decent reward.* So he went straight to the King and offered to bring his daughter back from the dead.

The King had heard that there was a discharged soldier going around returning the dead to life. He thought that Brother Scamp might be this man but he had his doubts. So he asked the advice of his counsellor, who said that, since his daughter was dead, he had nothing to lose.

Brother Scamp requested a cauldron of water and ordered everyone from the room. Then he severed the dead girl's limbs, chucked them into the water, and lit a fire exactly as he'd seen St Peter do. The water bubbled up. When the flesh fell away from the bones, he took them out and lay them on the table, like a puzzle; but he had no idea of the correct order and got the beautiful bones all jumbled up. Nevertheless, he stepped up to the table and cried, "In the name of the Holy Trinity, rise from the dead!" He said it three times more, but it was useless, and then he shouted, "Blasted girl! Get up off that table or I'll half-kill you!"

The words had no sooner left his mouth when St Peter came in through the window, once again disguised as a discharged soldier.

"Blasphemous godless man!" he yelled. "What

are you doing? How can the poor girl rise again when you've got her bones in such a pickle?"

"I've done the best I could, comrade," said Brother Scamp.

"I'll help you out just this once," said St Peter, "but if you ever try anything like this again, Heaven help you. Furthermore, you are neither to demand nor accept any reward from the King."

Then St Peter arranged the scrabble of bones in the right order and said three times, "In the name of the Holy Trinity, rise from the dead." The King's daughter breathed and sat up, as healthy and beautiful as she always was, and St Peter climbed out through the window. Brother Scamp was pleased things had worked out so well, but peeved at being forbidden to ask for his reward.

That bloke's not the full shilling, he thought. *What he gives with one hand he takes away with the other. It doesn't make sense.*

The King offered Brother Scamp any reward he wanted. He refused, as he'd been ordered to, but with hints, winks, nudges, shuffles and shrugs he got the King to fill his knapsack with gold and off he went.

St Peter was waiting at the palace gates. "Just look at you! Didn't I forbid you to accept anything? But, oh no. Out you march as bold as brass with your bag bulging with gold."

"I can't help it if they forced it on me," said Brother Scamp.

"You'd better not try this sort of thing again or you'll wish you hadn't."

"You needn't worry about that, Brother. Why should I bother to boil bones when I'm loaded with gold?"

"I can imagine how long your gold will last you," said St Peter. "But to keep you from meddling in forbidden ways again, I'll grant you the power to wish anything you want into your knapsack. Now goodbye to you. You will not see me again."

"Cheerio," said Brother Scamp and thought, *Good riddance more like, you peculiar person. I shan't be running to catch you up!* And he gave no more thought to the magical power of his knapsack.

Brother Scamp travelled on with his gold, and squandered, frittered and spent it the same as before. When he only had four shillings left, he came to an inn. *I might as well spend them,* he thought, and ordered up three shillings worth of wine and one of bread. He sat supping and the smell of roast goose teased his nostrils. When he looked around he saw two geese that the innkeeper was cooking in the oven. Suddenly he remembered that his companion had told him he could wish anything he wanted into his knapsack. *Oh ho!* he thought. *Let's see if it works with the geese.* He went outside and said, "I wish those two geese were out of the oven and in my knapsack!" After saying the words, he unbuckled the knapsack, peered in, and there they deliciously were. "This couldn't be better!" he said. "I'm a made man."

He sat down in a meadow and took out the geese. As he was busily eating, two journeymen came along and gawped hungrily at the goose that hadn't been touched yet. Brother Scamp thought to himself, *One goose is plenty for me,* and called over the two journeymen. "Here, take this goose and wish me well as you eat it."

They thanked him, went into the inn, ordered a flask of wine and a loaf of bread, took out

Brother Scamp's goose and began to eat. The innkeeper's wife had been watching them and said to her spouse, "That pair over there are guzzling a goose. Go and have a gander that it's not one of ours out of the oven."

He went and looked and the oven was worse than gooseless. "Hoy, you thieves! You think you're getting that goose pretty cheap, don't you? Pay up at once or I'll stripe your skins with a stick."

"We're not thieves," they protested. "A discharged soldier gave us the goose out there in the meadow."

"Don't try to pull the wool over my eyes," said the innkeeper. "There was a soldier here but he went out of that door empty-handed. I saw him myself. You're the thieves and you'd better pay up." But they couldn't pay, so he seized his stick and swiped them out of the inn.

Brother Scamp continued on his way and came to a place where there was a magnificent castle, and not far from it a wretched inn. He went to the inn and asked for a bed for the night, but the innkeeper refused him, saying, "There is no room. The house is full of noblemen."

Brother Scamp said, "That's odd. Why would they choose this place instead of that splendid castle?"

"Well, you see," said the inn-keeper, "it's not easy to spend a night in that castle. There's some that have tried, but none of them has ever come out alive."

"If others have tried, then so will I," said Brother Scamp.

"Don't even think about it," said the landlord. "It will be the end of you."

But Brother Scamp insisted, "Don't worry about me. Just give me the keys and something to eat and drink."

So the man gave him the keys and some bread and cheese and wine and Brother Scamp went into the castle and enjoyed his meal. After a while, he felt sleepy and lay down on the floor because there was no bed. He soon fell fast asleep, but in the middle of the night was awakened by a terrifying noise. When he opened his eyes, he saw nine ugly devils dancing round him in a circle.

"Dance as much as you like," said Brother Scamp, "but stay away from me." The devils came closer and closer and nearly stepped on his face with their hideous feet.

"Cut it out, you fiends!" he cried, but their frenzy got worse. Brother Scamp became very angry and shouted, "Shut up, I said!" He grabbed a table leg and set about them with it, but nine devils were too much for one soldier. While he was hitting the one in front of him, the ones behind him grabbed his hair and yanked fiercely. "Stinking devils! This is dreadful. But I'll show you something. All nine of you into my knapsack!" Wheesh! In they all went. He buckled the knapsack, flung it into a corner, and at last everything was still.

Brother Scamp lay down again and kipped until morning. The innkeeper and the nobleman who owned the castle arrived to see what had happened to him. They were astonished to find him alive and well and asked, "Didn't the ghosts harm you?"

"How could they harm me? I've got them all in my knapsack. Now you can live in your castle again. The ghosts won't bother you any more."

The nobleman thanked him, rewarded him extremely well, and begged him to stay in his service and he would provide for him till death. But Brother Scamp said, "No, I'm used to being footloose and fancy free. I'll just get on my way."

Back on the road, Brother Scamp stopped at a smithy, put the knapsack full of devils on the anvil, and asked the blacksmith and his apprentices to batter it with all their muscle. The devils screamed dreadfully, and when he opened the knapsack eight were dead, but one, who had cowered in a crease, was still alive. That one scuttled away and went straight to Hell.

After this, Brother Scamp travelled about for a long time, and if anyone knows what he got up to, they'll have a tale the length of a long road to tell. Finally, he grew old and his thoughts turned to death, so he went to a hermit who was respected as a Holy Man and said, "I'm tired of knocking about, and now I want to see about getting in to the Kingdom of Heaven."

The hermit replied, "There are two roads. One is broad and pleasant and leads to Hell. The other is narrow and rough and leads to Heaven."

Brother Scamp thought, *I'd be daft to take the rough and narrow way.* Sure enough, he took the broad, pleasant way and fetched up at a big black gate.

It was the Gate of Hell. He knocked and the gatekeeper squinted out to see who was there. When he saw Brother Scamp, he nearly leapt out of his scaly skin, for he just happened to be the ninth devil in the knapsack who'd escaped with only a black eye. Fast as a rat, he slammed, locked and bolted the gate, and fled to the Head Devil.

"There's a man outside with a knapsack," he said. "He wants to come in, but for Hell's sake don't let him, or he'll wish the lot of us into his knapsack. He had me in it once, and what a terrible battering I got!"

Brother Scamp was told he couldn't come in and should clear off. *If they won't give me a welcome here,* he thought, *I'll see if there's room for me in Heaven. I've got to stay somewhere.* So he turned around and travelled until he came to the Gate of Heaven, and knocked upon it. St Peter happened to be on duty as gatekeeper, and Brother Scamp recognized him right away. *Well, look who it is!* he thought. *My old comrade will be sure to give me a warmer reception.*

But St Peter said, "I don't believe it. You think you can get into Heaven?"

"Let me in, Brother, I've got to go somewhere. They wouldn't have me in Hell, or I'd not be stood here now."

"Too bad," said St Peter. "You're not coming in here."

"Well," said Brother Scamp, "if you really won't let me in then take back your knapsack, because I don't want to keep anything of yours."

"Hand it over then," said St Peter.

He passed the knapsack through the railings and St Peter hung it up behind his chair.

"Now," said Brother Scamp, "I wish myself into the knapsack."

Whoosh! There he was in the knapsack, the knapsack was in Heaven, and St Peter had to let him stay there – fair enough.

Rumpelstiltskin

Time was, there lived a miller who was very poor but he had one daughter more beautiful than any treasure. It happened one day that he met the King and to make himself seem special he boasted, "I have a daughter who can spin straw into gold."

This king was more than fond of gold, so he said to the miller, "That's a talent that would impress me enormously. If your daughter is as gifted as you say, bring her to my palace tomorrow and I'll put her to the test."

When the girl was brought to the King, he led her to a room that was full of straw, gave her a spinning-wheel and said, "Get going. You have all night ahead of you. But if you haven't spun all this straw into gold by dawn, you will die." Then he locked the door with his own hands and left her there alone.

The poor miller's daughter sat there without a clue what to do. She had no idea how to spin straw into gold and she grew more and more frightened and started to cry.

Suddenly the door opened and in leapt a little man who said, "Good evening, Mistress Miller. You're crying. Why?"

"Oh, I have to spin this straw into gold and I don't know how to do it."

"What will you give me if I do it for you?"

"My necklace."

"Done."

The little man palmed the necklace, squatted down before the spinning-wheel, and whirr, whirr, whirr! Three turns and the bobbin was full. And so he went on all night and at sunrise all the bobbins were lit with gold.

First thing in the morning, in swept the King and when he saw all the gold he was amazed and delighted. But the gold-greed grew in his heart and he had the miller's daughter taken to an even bigger room filled up with straw and told her to spin the lot into gold if she valued her life. She really didn't know what to do and was crying when the door opened again. In jumped the little man saying, "What will you give me if I spin all this straw into gold?"

"The ring from my finger."

"Done."

The little man pocketed the ring and whirred away at the wheel all the long dark night and by dawn each dull strand of straw was glistening gold. The King was beside himself with pleasure at the treasure, but his desire for gold still wasn't satisfied. He took the miller's daughter to an even larger room stuffed with straw and told her, "You must spin all of this into gold tonight and if you do I shall make you my wife." And the King said to himself, "She's only the miller's daughter, but I won't find a wealthier wench in the world!"

As soon as the girl was alone, the little man appeared for the third time and said, "What will you give me this time if I spin the straw into gold for you?"

"I have nothing left to give."

"Then you must swear to give me the first child you have after you are Queen."

Who knows what the future will bring, thought the girl. And as she had no choice, she promised and gave her word to the little man. At once he started to spin until all the straw was pure gold.

When the King arrived in the morning and saw the room bulging with gold, he held the wedding that very day and the miller's beautiful daughter became Queen.

After a year she brought a gorgeous golden child into the world and thought no more of the little man. But one day he bounced suddenly into her room and said, "Now give me what you promised me."

The Queen was truly horrified and offered him all the gold and riches of the kingdom if he would only leave her child. But the little man said, "No. I'd rather have a warm and living child than the largest, hardest diamond in the world." Hearing this, the Queen began to sob so bitterly that the little man took pity on her and said, "I'll give you three days. If you can find out my name by then, you can keep your child."

The Queen sat up all night, searching her brains for his name like someone sieving for gold. She went through every single name she could think of. She sent out a messenger to ask everywhere in the land for all the names that could be spoken, sung or spelled. On the next day, when the little man came, she recited the whole alphabet of names that she'd learned, starting with Balthasar, Casper, Melchior . . . But to each one the little man piped, "That's not my name."

On the second day, she sent servants all round the neighbourhood to ferret out more names and she tried all the weird and wacky ones on the little man. "Perhaps you're called Shortribs or Sheepshanks or Lacelegs."

But he always said, "That's not my name."

On the third day, the messenger came back and said, "I haven't managed to find a single new name, but as I came near to a high mountain at the end of forest, the place where fox and hare wish each other goodnight, I spied a small hut. There was a fire burning outside it and round the flames danced a bizarre little man. He hopped on one leg and bawled,

"Bake today! Tomorrow brew!
Then I'll take the young Queen's child!
She will cry and wish she knew
That RUMPELSTILTSKIN's how I'm
styled."

You can imagine how overjoyed the Queen was when she heard the name. And when, soon afterwards, the little man stalked in and demanded, "Well, Mistress Queen, what is my name?" She started by saying,

"Is it Tom?"

"No."

"Is it Dick?"

"No."

"Is it Harry?"

"No."

"Maybe your name is Rumpelstiltskin?"

"The devil has told you! The devil has told you!" shrieked the little man. In his rage he stamped his right foot so hard on the ground that it went right in up to his middle. And then in a fury he pulled at his left leg so hard with the very same hands that had spun the straw into gold that he tore himself in two. In two!

The Magic Table, the Gold-Donkey and the Cudgel in the Sack

It happened once that there was a tailor who had three sons and one goat. The goat provided milk for the four of them, so every day it had to be taken out to graze, and fed well. The sons took turns in doing this. One day, the eldest lad took the goat to the churchyard. There was lots of excellent greenery there and he let her graze and jump around and generally play the goat. At dusk, when it was time to go home, he asked her, "Goat, have you had enough to eat?"

And the goat replied,

"I've had enough,
I'm full of the stuff. Beh! Beh!"

"Let's go home then," said the boy, and he took hold of her halter, led her back to her shed and tied her up safely.

"Well," said his father, "did you feed our goat properly?"

"Oh, yes," said his son, "she's had enough; she's full of the stuff."

But his father wanted to check for himself, so he went down to the shed, patted his precious goat, and enquired, "Goat, are you sure you've had enough to eat?"

The goat replied:

"There was no grass to eat
Where he took me to feed,
Hard stones on the ground
Were all that I found. Beh! Beh!"

"What's this I hear!" thundered the tailor. He ran back up and said to his eldest son, "You liar! Why did you tell me you'd given the goat enough to eat when you've let her starve?" In his fury, he grabbed his yardstick from the wall and thrashed his son right out of the house.

Next day, it was the second son's turn. He picked a good place by the garden hedge with lots of fresh, succulent greenery, and the goat chomped it right down to the ground. At home-

time, the boy asked, "Goat, have you had enough
to eat?" and the goat answered,

"I've had enough,
I'm full of the stuff. Beh! Beh!"

"Let's get home then," said the boy, and he led
her back and tied her securely in the shed.

"Well," said his father, "did you feed the goat
well?"

"No problem," said his son. "She's had enough;
she's full of the stuff."

But the tailor went down to the shed to make sure, and said, "Goat, have you had enough to eat?"

The goat answered,

"There was no grass to eat
Where he took me to feed,
Hard stones on the ground
Were all that I found. Beh! Beh!"

"The heartless big lump!" yelled the tailor. "Letting such a fine animal starve!" And he ran up and seized his stick and thwacked his poor son out of the house.

Now it was the youngest son's turn, and he was determined to do things properly. He chose a spot bursting with bushes and greenery and let the goat nibble away to her heart's content. In the evening, he asked, "Goat, are you quite, quite sure you've had enough?"

The goat replied,

"I've had enough,
I'm full of the stuff. Beh! Beh!"

"Let's go home then," said the boy, and he

led her to her shed and tied her up.

"Well," asked his father, "have you fed the goat properly?"

"Yes," said this son, "she's had enough; she's full of the stuff."

But the tailor didn't trust him, and went down to ask, "Goat, are you sure you've had enough to eat?"

And the wicked goat said,

"There was no grass to eat
Where he took me to feed,
Hard stones on the ground
Were all that I found. Beh! Beh!"

"You pack of liars!" roared the tailor. "All three of you are deceitful and undutiful. Well, you'll not make a fool out of me any more!" And quite purple in the face with rage, he rushed up and beat the poor youngest boy's back with the stick so hard that he ran out of the house.

Now the old tailor was all alone with his goat. Next morning, he went down to the shed, stroked the goat and said, "Come along, my little pet, I'll take you out to graze myself." He led her away to a place where there were green hedges and moist grasses and all the things goats love to eat. "Now you can eat your fill for once," he said, and let her chomp away till evening. Then he asked, "Dear goat, have you had enough to eat"

And the goat replied,

"I've had enough,
I'm full of the stuff. Beh! Beh!"

"Come along home then," said the tailor; and he led her to her shed and tied her up. As he was leaving, he turned round and said, "Now for once I *know* you've really had plenty to eat."

But he had no more luck with the goat than his poor sons had had, for the bad goat bleated out,

"There was no grass to eat
Where you took me to feed,
Hard stones on the ground
Were all that I found. Beh! Beh!"

When the tailor heard this, he was horrified

174

and realized how unjustly he'd treated his three sons. "You ungrateful beast!" he screamed at the goat. "Just you wait! I'll make a mark on you that'll stop you showing your treacherous face amongst decent folk!" He rushed upstairs, grabbed his razor, lathered the goat's head, and shaved it as smooth as a billiard-ball. And because the stick would have been too good for her, he fetched his whip and flogged her so badly that she went leaping away for her life.

So the tailor was now all alone in his empty house. He became terribly sad and longed to have his sons back again, but nobody knew where they were. The eldest boy had become a joiner's apprentice. He was hard-working and conscientious; and when his apprenticeship was over and it was time for him to move on, his master gave him a little table. It was made of oak and looked quite ordinary, but there was something special about it. If you put it before you and said, "Table, be laid!" this splendid little table would immediately cover itself with a clean tablecloth, and there would be a plate with a knife and fork, as many dishes of good hot food as there was room for, and a big, robust, glowing glass of ruby wine to warm the frostiest heart. The young man thought to himself, *Now you've got enough for your whole life*, and he journeyed happily round the world. He didn't have to bother whether any inn he came to was good, bad or indifferent, or whether or not he could find a decent meal. Sometimes, if he was in the mood, he didn't even stay at an inn but camped out in the fields and woods. He'd take the table from his back, put it in front of him and say, "Table, be laid!" and it gave him all the food and drink he wanted.

Eventually, the lad decided to return home to his father. He thought, *He won't be angry with me after all this time; and now that I have a magic table, he's sure to welcome me!* So he set off home, and one evening he came to an inn that was full of guests. They made him welcome and asked him to join them at their meal, otherwise there'd be no food left for him. "No," said the young joiner, "I won't take your last few mouthfuls. You shall be my guests instead."

They thought he was joking with them and they laughed. But he set down his table in the centre of the room and said, "Table, be laid!" At once, it was covered with much better food than the landlord of the inn could even dream of, and the delicious smell of it made all their noses twitch like rabbits. "Help yourselves, mates," said the joiner, and they all scraped up their chairs, grasped their knives and forks, and tucked in, grinning. The amazing thing was that as soon as one dish was empty, another full one took its place, quicker than a burp.

The landlord stood watching silently from a corner. *I could do with a cook like that here at my inn*, he thought. The joiner and his guests ate and drank and laughed and talked late into the night. But at last they went to bed; and the young man lay down to sleep as well, putting his magic table against the wall. The landlord's envy kept him awake like hunger. He remembered that he had a table which looked exactly the same up in his attic. So very quietly he fetched it, crept in, and swapped it for the magic table.

Next morning, the joiner paid his bill, lifted the table on to his back – never dreaming that it was the wrong one – and headed off for his father's house. He arrived home at midday and his father was overjoyed to see him.

"Well, well, well, my dear boy," he said. "What have you learnt?"

"Father, I've become a joiner."

"That's a worthwhile trade," replied his father, "and what have you brought back with you from your travels?"

"Father, I've brought the most wonderful thing – a little table."

The old man examined the table all over and said, "Well, you've made no work of art here. It's just a shabby old table."

"But it's a magic table," said the son. "When I put it down in front of me and tell it to lay itself, the finest food and wine appear and gladden the heart. Just ask all our friends and relations over and we'll give them a night to remember. They can scoff and quaff as much as they want."

So when all the guests had assembled, he put

his little table in the middle of the room and said, "Table, be laid!" But this table did nothing. It stayed just as bare and wooden and still as any other table that doesn't understand it's being spoken to. Then the poor joiner realized what had happened at the inn, and he stood there ashamed and embarrassed that they'd all think he was a liar. His relations had a good old laugh at him, but had to go home with empty stomachs. His father got out some cloth and went on tailoring, and the boy found work with a master joiner.

The second son had fetched up at a mill and apprenticed himself to the miller. When he'd finished his time, his master said, "Because you've been such a good worker, I'm going to give you a donkey. He's very special. He doesn't pull a cart and he won't carry sacks of flour either."

"Then what's the use of him?" asked the young man.

"He spits out gold," said the miller. "If you stand him on a cloth and say 'Jobaloo', this magnificent beast will produce gold coins for you from both ends!"

"This is wonderful," said the young man.

He thanked his master and set off into the world. If ever he needed gold, he only had to say "Jobaloo" to his donkey. Out would pump a jackpot of gold coins and he just had to bend down and scrabble them up. Because his purse was always bulging with gold, he bought the best of everything. After travelling for a while, he decided to visit his father. He thought, *When I turn up with the gold-donkey, he'll forget his anger and welcome me home.*

On his way home, he stopped at the same inn as his brother. He was leading his donkey, and the landlord was about to take it for him, when he said, "No problem, landlord. I'll take my donkey to the stable myself. I like to know where he is." The landlord thought this was odd, and that a man who had to tie up his own donkey wasn't likely to have much money to spend. But when the young man pulled two gold pieces from his pocket and told him to buy something good for supper, the landlord's eyes gaped like an empty purse and he sped away to buy the best food and drink. After dinner, his guest asked him if he owed him anything, and the greedy landlord thought he might as well charge double and asked for two more gold pieces.

The boy put his hand in his pocket, but it was empty, so he said, "Hang on, landlord, I'll just go and fetch some more gold." But he took the tablecloth with him.

The landlord couldn't understand this at all, so he sleekitly followed the boy. He crept along and discovered that his guest had bolted the stable door. Filled with curiosity, he peeped in through a gap in the wood. The young man spread the tablecloth under the donkey, called out "Jobaloo" and suddenly the beast began to throw out gold from both ends – showers and showers of it.

"Well, who would believe it?" said the land-lord, rubbing his eyes in astonishment. "That's the fastest way I've seen to make gold. I could use a money-mule like that!"

The young man paid for his meal and went to bed; but the landlord sneaked down to the stables overnight, led the gold-donkey away and tied up another donkey in its place.

Early next morning, the boy set off, thinking he still led his own gold-donkey. He arrived home at midday and his father gave him a warm welcome.

"Well, well, well, my boy, and what have you become?"

"I am a miller, Father."

"And what have you brought back with you from your travels?"

"Just a donkey."

"We're all right for donkeys round here," said the father. "It would have been better if you'd bought a decent goat."

"But this isn't just a normal donkey, Father, it's a gold-donkey. When I say 'Jobaloo', this wonderful creature drops down a whole tablecloth of gold coins. Ask all our friends and relatives round and I'll make every one of them rich."

"That'll suit me," said the tailor. "I won't need to work my old fingers to the bone with this needle any more." And he ran round himself and invited all their relations.

As soon as everyone was there, the son asked them to clear a space, spread out a cloth and led in the donkey. "Watch this everybody!" he said proudly, and called out "Jobaloo!" But what plopped and steamed on the white cloth was certainly not gold, and it was obvious that this donkey could produce no more than any other smelly old donkey. The poor young miller was mortified and felt like a complete ass. He knew that he'd been hoodwinked and just had to apologize to his relatives, who trudged home as poor as they'd always been. So the old man had to take up his needle again and the boy had to get a job with a miller.

The youngest son had apprenticed himself to a turner, and because this is such a skilled trade, he took longest to learn it. His brothers wrote him a letter telling him of their bad luck and how a villainous landlord had nicked their magic gifts on the night before they got home. When the young turner had completed his time and was setting out to travel, his master rewarded him for his fine, honest work with a sack. "It's got a cudgel inside," he said.

"Well, I can sling the sack over my shoulder and make good use of it," said the boy, "but the cudgel will just make it heavy to carry. What use is it?"

"Plenty use," said his master. "If anyone ever does you any harm at all, just say 'Cudgel, out of the sack!' and the cudgel will jump out at whoever's there and dance so madly on their backs that they won't be able to walk for a week. And it won't stop till you say 'Cudgel, back in the sack!'"

The young miller said thank you, slung the sack over his shoulder, and after that, if anyone gave him any trouble, he'd say "Cudgel, out of the sack!" At once the cudgel would leap out and give their coats or jackets such a fierce dust-ing – while they were still wearing them – and it

184

hammered their backs so fast that before the next man knew what was happening it was his turn already.

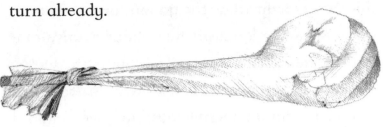

Eventually, the boy arrived at the bad landlord's inn. He put his sack down in front of him on the table, and started to talk about all the miraculous things he'd seen on his travels. "Oh yes," he yawned, "you come across magic tables and gold-donkeys and all that sort of thing – excellent in their way and I've nothing against them – but they're nothing compared to the treasure I've got in my sack here."

The landlord listened excitedly and wondered what it could be. He thought, *Perhaps his sack is filled with jewels. If it is, I should have them as well. Twice is nice, but thrice is nicer.*

At bedtime, the boy lay down on the bench and put his sack under his head for a pillow. When the landlord thought he was sound asleep, he sneaked up and began tugging very gently and slowly at the sack. His sly plan was to pull it out and put another one in its place. Of course, this was exactly what the young turner wanted, and just as the landlord was about to give one last tug, he called out, "Cudgel, out of the sack!"

Faster than rage, the cudgel was out and giving the landlord a terrible dusting. The landlord screamed and howled but the more noise he made, the more the cudgel danced and stomped on his back, till finally he fell to the ground and stayed there.

Then the young man said, "Unless you give back the magic table and the gold-donkey, the cudgel's cha-cha will begin again."

"Oh, no," moaned the landlord – very humbly now – "I'll give you the lot, sir, honestly, just tell that hideous thing to get back in its sack."

"Very well, I shall give you mercy as well as justice," said the young man, "but just you mind your step in future." Then he called out, "Cudgel, back in the sack!" and the cudgel had a well-earned rest.

Next morning, the turner went home to his father with the magic table and the gold-

186

donkey. His father was delighted to see him, and asked him what he had learnt.

"I am a turner, Father," he said.

"A very skilful trade," said the old tailor. "And what have you brought back from your travels?"

"Something very valuable, Father. A cudgel in a sack."

"A cudgel?" scoffed his father. "What for? You can hack one off the nearest tree."

The son smiled. "Not one like this, dear Father; when I say 'Cudgel, out of the sack!' the cudgel jumps out and bangs away at anyone who's giving me grief. And it doesn't stop its bruising dance until they beg for mercy. Look, Father, with this wonderful cudgel I've got back the magic table and the gold-donkey that were pinched from my brothers. So send for both of them and invite all our friends and relations. I'll fill their bellies with food and drink and their pockets with gold."

The old tailor still wasn't sure about this, but he did as his youngest son asked.

When they were all together, the turner put a cloth down on the floor, led in the gold-donkey, and said to his brother, "Now, my dear Brother, speak to your donkey!"

The miller called out "Jobaloo!" and there and then it began to hail gold coins on the cloth. The donkey didn't stop till everyone's pockets were bulging (I bet you wish you'd been there as well!).

Then the turner fetched the little table and said, "Speak to your table, my good Brother."

As soon as the joiner cried "Table be laid!" the table was crowded with every delicious dish and the best wine. Then they had a feast the like of which had never been dreamed of in the poor tailor's house, and the whole family stayed together till late at night, having the most wonderful party. The tailor packed away his needle and thread and yardstick, and lived long and happy and prosperous with his three fine sons.

But what about that wicked goat whose fault it was that the three boys had been thrown out of their home? Listen to this. She was so ashamed of being bald that she ran to a fox-hole and crawled in to hide there. When the fox came home, he saw two huge yellowy eyes gleaming

at him in the darkness. He was so scared that he ran away.

The bear met him and the fox looked so terrified that he asked, "What's up, brother fox?"

"Oh," said the fox. "There's a terrible monster sitting in my earth-hole, glowering at me with glowing eyes."

"We'll soon get rid of it," said the bear, and he went with the fox to his hole and peeped in. But when he saw the fiery eyes, he was scared as well, and ran away.

The bee met him, and saw that he looked upset and said, "Bear, you look ill with worry. What's up?"

"Oh, it's awful," said the bear. "There's a murderous beast with burning eyes sitting in brother fox's house and we can't get it out."

The bee said, "Poor old bear. I know I'm only a wee thing that you hardly ever notice, but I think I can help you."

The bee flew into the fox's hole, landed on the goat's bald head and stung her so badly that she leapt up bleating "Beh! Beh! Beh!" and clattered out into the big wide world like a mad thing. And nobody knows or cares where she ran from that day to this.